THE LADY AND THE PIRATE
Queenmakers Saga VI

BY
BERNADETTE ROWLEY

THE LADY AND THE PIRATE
Bernadette Rowley
Copyright © 2020 Bernadette Rowley
All rights reserved.

First published 2017 by Bernadette Rowley
Second publication 2019 by Bernadette Rowley

ISBN: 978-0-6483105-7-0

Printing/manufacturing information for this book may be found on the last page

First Printing 2017 by Bernadette Rowley
Second Printing 2020 by Bernadette Rowley
2020 Cover Design by Dar Albert
Interior Design by
Business Communications Management bcm-online.com.au

VC:TLTP-20200624

ACKNOWLEDGEMENTS

To Louise Cusack for her inspiration and advice
over the last ten years.

To Duncan Carling-Rodgers for his editing and formatting skills
and so much more.

To my husband, Michael, and my sons for their unending love and
support and for sharing in the disappointments and
triumphs of a writing life.

Titles by
Bernadette Rowley

(in suggested reading order)

Princess Avenger - Queenmakers Saga I

The Lady's Choice - Queenmakers Saga II

Princess in Exile - Queenmakers Saga III

The Lord and the Mermaid - Queenmakers Saga IV

The Elf King's Lady - Queenmakers Saga V

The Lady and the Pirate - Queenmakers Saga VI

The Master and the Sorceress - Queenmakers Saga VII

Elf Princess Warrior - Queenmakers Saga VIII

DEDICATION

Dedicated to the memory of my mother-in-law,
Esther Rowley.

TABLE OF CONTENTS

CHAPTER 1

"CAPTAIN, you're needed above."

Esta shook off the nightmare and sat up in her bunk, trying to shake the dread that clung to her. "What's the problem?"

"We have a visitor." Stino, her first mate, turned and left her cabin, closing the door behind him.

She drew a deep and heavy sigh, her heart kicking up a notch as she contemplated who the visitor might be. On a ship, miles out to sea at night, there were few possibilities and none of them good.

She tossed back the blankets and stood. After straightening her black breeches and blue satin shirt, she donned the heavy blue cloak and made sure her wig, bandanna and mask were in place. When she opened her door, Stino was waiting in the corridor.

"Who is it?" she asked.

"I don't know, Captain. Just said you were to come quick like. He has dark elves with him."

Her stomach clenched and a tide of bile rose to her throat. That could only mean one thing. She had dreaded it for as long as she had been beating up and down the coast in her ship. She followed Stino along the corridor and up the ladder. He stepped to the side and stood at attention as she emerged onto the main deck.

The vibrant green eyes of their visitor froze Esta in place. He was a big man, taller than average, well-muscled and with short brown hair and a scruffy beard. Her breath caught in her throat, but she quickly took herself in hand. Her crew was spread out over the deck and all were armed. There was no reason to feel intimidated despite the six dark-skinned elves who accompanied him. They were a tall, lithe people with characteristic pointed ears and oval pupils. Her gaze flicked out to starboard. The fog had lifted, and a larger ship lay at anchor.

She looked back at the man. "The Singing Pirate, I presume?"

"My reputation precedes me, Madam." He smiled but his eyes narrowed. "A pity it is that I can't say the same."

Stino growled. "You're in the presence of Lady Moonlight, Sir, and I would caution you to show more respect or the lads and I might teach you some."

Esta touched Stino's arm to calm him and looked at their guest. "What is it you want, pirate?"

"Whatever you carry that's of value. Make it quick and I may spare your lives." He stood with arms folded, feet apart, his tan breeches molding the muscles of powerful thighs. A niggle began at the back of her consciousness; he looked familiar.

"Have we met before?" she asked.

The pirate stepped toward her and Stino growled again but the larger man ignored her crewman. He reached for her chin and turned it this way and that, then ran his fingers down her cheek beside the mask.

She shivered.

"I don't think so, I would've remembered." The gravelly timbre of his voice played with her nerves. "What do you carry?"

Esta swallowed three times before she could be certain her voice would work. Even then it came out too breathy. "We have wool and skins."

He frowned. "Too bulky, what else?"

She steeled herself not to show the nerves that tightened her belly, and deliberately relaxed her shoulders. "Fine wine from the northern mountains."

"Still no good. I want high value, low bulk. I'll not leave empty-handed."

"A pity you came then, pirate," she said.

As he eyed her up and down, anger flared bright and sharp in her chest. She clenched her fists. Oh, to teach this arrogant wretch a lesson he'd never forget.

Where is Katrine when I need her?

"I never leave a ship without bounty," he said. "If you have none, then *you* will have to do." He stepped closer and seized her arm. The sound of twenty cutlasses being drawn sliced through her.

The elves had nocked arrows trained on the closest of her men.

"Call your men off, Lady Moonlight, or they'll be slaughtered."

Stino placed the tip of his cutlass at the pirate's neck and was repaid by an arrow through his chest. He dropped to the deck.

"Stino!" Esta tried to wrench her arm from the pirate's grip but the man had a hand of steel.

"You're mine now," he growled. "All loyalties must be put aside including any you feel for your unfortunate crewman."

She met his steely gaze with one of her own. "I'll *never* be yours. Leave this ship now."

A fireball blazed down from above and hit the deck at their feet. Heat flashed up and she lurched backward, suddenly free.

At last she decides to help!

More fireballs landed near them, one striking an elf and setting his clothes afire. He dived over the side of the ship, closely followed by his five comrades. The fire died.

The Singing Pirate glared at her, his teeth bared. "I see you have black magic at your disposal!"

"Leave now and never return." She drew herself up. "This ship is defended, and you would do well to remember."

The pirate stalked to the starboard rail and turned back to her. "You've not seen the last of me." He climbed over the side, clutched a grappling hook that no doubt secured a line down to his rowboat, and vanished.

Esta dropped to her knees beside Stino and grasped his hand. His chest barely moved and the light in his eyes had dimmed. "I'm sorry. I'll ensure your wife and son are taken care of."

"I know you will, My Lady." His head sagged to the side and she felt for a pulse, though knew in her heart that he had passed.

Shiny black boots appeared beside her and she looked up. Katrine, her younger sister, stood there. She was a beauty with long dark hair, intelligent blue eyes and more than enough attitude. She was also a witch.

"How is he?" Katrine asked.

Esta closed Stino's eyes. She couldn't help the tear that trickled down her cheek. "Dead."

"And the pirate?"

"Over the side." Esta stood and walked to the rail, spying a vague splash that must have been the pirate's rowboat. "The *Lenweri* went first and then their master. What do you make of it?"

"He's a traitor to the kingdom, associating with the elves like that," Katrine said. "Even pirates should know better."

"You took your sweet time, Sister," Esta said, eyeing Katrine. "I was mere moments from being seized as that man's plunder." She shivered at the thought of his hands on her.

"I would never have let him take you and was merely waiting to see what would happen. I thought perhaps your men could handle a few elves," Katrine snapped. "What shall we do with Stino?"

Esta sighed. "As we're on the home run, we'll bind his body and convey it to his widow."

Katrine's eyes softened. "I'll take care of that if you like."

Esta squared her shoulders and met her sister's gaze. "No, I'll face his widow."

Katrine stiffened. "I'm quite capable, you know."

"It's my duty." She returned to Stino's body and crossed his hands over his chest. He appeared almost peaceful now. Her heart bled at the thought of what she must do, but if she allowed Katrine to complete this distasteful task the widow would think her a coward. Esta had never been that.

** * **

Samael Delacost lay on the deck of his ship, *Silver Lady*, gasping and struggling to understand what the hell had just happened.

Black magic, that's what!

Ten years a pirate and still this life had the ability to surprise. But the woman - she was the biggest surprise. He had wanted to bring her with him and that could never be allowed to happen. Women only complicated life aboard ship, although his *Lenweri* were immune to human females.

Nande, the dark elf who was his second-in-command, appeared before him as Sam dragged himself to his feet.

"I have heard what transpired, Captain, and I wish to apologize for my *Lenweri*." Nande's unblinking gaze showed no emotion. "The five remaining from the mission will be punished."

"Don't be too hard on them, Nande. There was a witch on board that ship." He ran his hands through his hair. "Who did we lose?"

"Lile has gone to his reward, Captain," Nande said. "He never reached the *Silver Lady*."

Sam nodded, the ache in his heart unexpected. "We'll head home so you can convey the news to his family."

Nande shook his head and the elves with him looked indifferent. "His kin disowned him when he took to the sea. They will not care that he is dead."

Sam nodded again. It was Lile's choice to follow him and to volunteer to be part of the boarding party. The young elf had known the risks. Still, the *Lenweri* were Sam's family, apart from his parents, and it hurt to lose one. Perhaps it was time to visit his mother and father, so they knew *their* son was alive.

"Then let's hoist sail for home, and on the way, we'll drink to our friend Lile who left us this night."

The elves all nodded and quietly went about their tasks, while Sam sat staring at the faint lights on the retreating ship. He looked forward to his next encounter with her ladyship.

Chapter 2

ESTA sat at her desk in the library, working with ink and quill on the estate figures. No matter how she tallied them, the numbers told her next month would be difficult. A certain devilish man kept intruding into her thoughts, the memory of his compelling eyes sending shivers down her spine. She had tallied the column before her three times and come to as many different answers.

A bell tinkled from within the house.

"Damn bell," she muttered. "One day I swear I'll throw that thing off a cliff." She pushed up from her desk and left the room in search of her mother.

"What is it, Mother?" she asked when she reached the sunny chamber her mother occupied.

"It's time to get the fire laid and bring me my dinner, girl. While you're at it, these bed socks have a hole."

Esta sighed, pushing strands of hair out of her eyes. "Where's your maid?"

"I sent her home, poor thing. She has the sniffles. Besides, only you can darn my socks the way I like."

Anger started a slow burn in Esta's gut. She loved her mother, but sometimes…

"Mother, I'd appreciate it if you could get your maid to do as much as possible. I have the estate to run and the bills won't pay themselves."

"Too busy for your own mother now, are you? When I think of all the years I slaved to raise you and your sister…"

The sharp pang of guilt hit where it always did - right on target. Esta was the oldest daughter. She owed her mother a comfortable life. It was just... some days she longed for more. Her thoughts drifted back to the Singing Pirate and the enticing way his shoulders had filled his tunic. He had said they would meet again. She shivered.

"I told you it was time to set the fire," her mother said, rousing her from her reverie.

Esta sighed and began stacking the logs from the wood box into the fireplace.

* * *

Sam tethered his skiff to the jetty and headed into the town of Costa. It had been his home for thirty-two years, if anywhere but his ship could be called thus. He entered his favorite dockside tavern as a worker was lighting the street lanterns. The glow gave the docks a welcoming feel. He took a deep breath of air filled with brine, dead fish and stale ale. Not the fresh smell of the ocean, but a damned sight better than the putrid stench of the alleys further into town.

He pulled his cap down over his eyes and pushed through the door, heading straight for a corner seat, in order to have a wall at his back. He ordered ale and a plate of eggs and relaxed in his chair, eyes closed. You could pick up a lot if you closed your eyes; tuned into the sounds around you.

Sometimes juicy titbits of information led to a bounty on its way up or down the coast. Other times, he had been alerted to naval patrols that might otherwise have netted the Singing Pirate.

Tonight, there was only town gossip: a new babe for the barman's daughter, a census being called for by the mayor and a string of robberies since he had last docked. There was little to attract his interest until he heard a mention of his parents

"Wretched thing yearning for a child," an older man near the fire said. "I remember our neighbors Harah and Claus. They were a devoted young couple but so sad. Until the day a girl showed up with a newborn. They took the babe on and he grew up with loving parents. Went a bit wild. Haven't seen him for years."

Sam's chest tightened; breath frozen in his lungs. His parents with another woman's child? What had become of that child, that son? It couldn't be him, could it?

A great yawning chasm opened within, and he pushed up from the table. Throwing coins down, he stumbled toward the door, knocking over chairs and pushing past patrons at the bar. He gained the door and gulped huge breaths of cold air, curses drifting to him from the men he had disturbed. He stood there until his head cleared and the spinning stopped, then headed up the hill.

Sam had barely brushed his knuckles across the door before it opened and he was drawn into his parents' welcoming but modest parlor.

"Samael, son," Claus Delacost said, shaking his hand before closing and bolting the door behind him. "It's been so long; I had started to wonder… Never mind, it's good to see you."

He swallowed twice before he had his voice under control. These people were his family. The only family he had. It couldn't be true.

"Here I am, large as life, and I've brought you something to make life easier." He drew out three gold coins from his pocket and his father's eyes widened.

"I won't take them if they're stolen, Samael, you know how I feel about that." Claus shoved his hands into his pockets, staring at the coins in Sam's outstretched hand.

"For Mother, then," he said. "We nearly lost her last year when you ran out of coin for firewood and she took a chill. Put it away for times of need."

Claus took the offered coin and crossed to the fireplace where he removed a block, tucked the coins into an alcove and replaced the stone. He turned back to Sam. "Thank you."

"Sammy, oh dear Goddess you're alive." Harah Delacost threw herself into Sam's arms and her tears soaked his shoulder.

How could he begin this conversation, when he received a welcome like this? These people loved him and yet he could destroy them if he asked the questions that burned within. He hugged his mother tight until the storm of weeping settled and her trembling eased.

Should he bury his doubts and act as if nothing had happened? It couldn't be true. If it was, did he really want to confront something that could shatter the very basis of his life until this point? No, he didn't. He would enjoy a night with his parents and not say anything to pull apart the small family he treasured. But even as he reached that decision, something inside pushed at him to discover the truth, not to let sleeping dogs lie. He drew both his parents closer to the fire. "Sit, please."

His parents looked at each other and slowly took their seats. Why did they appear so fearful? Was it true? Had they harbored this secret for thirty-two years? He shook his head, gritting his teeth to suppress the words that fought their way to his lips, still unsure he should say anything. The rumors were probably lies. If so, there was nothing to fear.

"I've a matter I wish to discuss."

"That sounds serious," Claus said.

Sam stood before them, head down, searching the rushes on the floor for the words he needed. The seconds dragged into minutes while he discarded first one question and then another.

"Spit it out, Samael," Claus snapped. "Whatever it is, we will deal with it."

Sam hoped that was the case, because he could be about to erase everything he had thought of as truth in the most critical relationship in his life.

He looked at his mother. "Did you birth me?"

Harah's eyes grew wide as she drew a sharp breath. "Why do you ask?"

"Just answer the question, Mother," he snapped. "You owe me that!"

Claus leapt to his feet. "We don't owe you a damned thing, Samael Delacost. We have loved you like our own all these years and won't be judged for it."

He staggered back at his father's admission. A part of him had believed it was all a hideous mistake. "So it's true? You adopted me?"

Harah reached for Claus's hand. Suddenly, she appeared frail. "I love you Sammy. No birth mother could ever love you more."

He hardened his heart to her grief. He had to if he wished to ask the questions he needed to. "How old was I when I came to you?"

Harah had started weeping again so Claus told the tale. "You were only a few weeks old when your mother came to us. She had born you out of wedlock and her parents had shunned her. She couldn't support a child and so did the only thing she could. Somehow she heard we were barren and came knocking."

Harah stood before him. "We couldn't believe our good fortune. Someone had offered us a perfect son to brighten our days. We didn't hesitate once it was clear how desperate her situation was. Your father investigated the girl's circumstances and she told the truth."

"What was her name?" Sam asked.

"Vitavia," Harah said. "I never knew her last name or that of the father."

"A beautiful name," he murmured.

"She had already named you, so we kept that part of your heritage," Claus said.

"Little enough of her, I had," he snapped, unbearably bitter at the thought his mother had handed him to strangers and walked out of his life. "What am I supposed to make of this?"

"You accept it and move on," Claus said. "No point in bitterness."

"Easy for you to say," he said. "I assume you know where *you* came from."

"What difference does it make?" Claus asked. "The only thing that matters is what you make of your life."

Sam shook his head. "All my life I've felt I was on the outside looking in. I've always blamed being poor and having to struggle to make ends meet. Now I wonder if it was because I was abandoned."

Harah sat and put her head in her hands. "I worried this day would come," she said. "I agonized over whether we should tell you, but each time it seemed too difficult. Would it have helped, Sam?"

"I'd love to say no, Mother, but knowing earlier might have made the next step easier."

"Sam," Claus said, his tone closer to anger than Sam had ever heard it, "I won't see you hurt your mother by trying to find that girl!"

"Don't you see, Father? That girl is my mother. I may have brothers and sisters out there. I need to do this before I *can* go forward." He knelt before the only woman who had ever really loved him. "I don't wish to hurt you, Mother, but you do understand how much it would mean to me to find my family, don't you?"

Harah nodded, her grey eyes watery and incredibly sad. "I should have planned for this day and I'm sorry it was such a shock. Go and find her and may the Goddess be with you."

Sam hugged her close, feeling the invisible string that bound their hearts grow tighter. She would always be his mother, no matter what came to pass. He stood, shook his father's hand and left without another word.

CHAPTER 3

ESTA drew the small chest toward her as the rain beat down on the windowpane. It was a disgusting, dreary day. The perfect opportunity to examine some of the more obscure objects from her last two forays up the coast. She loved delving into boxes and unwrapping the cloth from pieces, wondering what she would find. More often than not it was junk: a child's favorite bauble or a worthless statue.

The chest was the last item to be examined. Its flimsy lock wasn't difficult to remove, and she lifted the lid. It was dry inside. Papers lay on top and beneath them was a cow skin map. Centuries of wear had thinned the leather and a piece snapped off the edge as she lifted it out.

Under the map, was a personal history book, complete with family trees and dates of births, deaths and marriages - the family name wasn't familiar. Deeper in the chest, was an object wrapped in linen. It was hard and heavy. Her heart raced as she uncovered an intricately engraved metal rod. None of the runes made any sense. She touched it with her finger and a zap of something reached out, burning her.

"Ouch!" she said, placing the injured digit in her mouth. She dropped the rod on the desk in its linen wrap and called for Katrine.

"What is it now?" her sister snapped as she entered the room a few minutes later. "Mother is being unbearable and as soon as I take leave from her unending demands, *you* call for me."

Esta pulled her finger from her mouth and studied her sister. Sometimes it was easy to forget Katrine was only two years younger.

"You won't be sorry, dear," she said. "Look at the rod on the desk and tell me what you think."

Katrine frowned and moved closer. She reached out her right palm and swept it through the air above the object. She looked at it from one side and then the other before muttering the words of a spell.

"Interesting." She picked up the rod with her bare hands. "It was warded with a protection spell, though it would be ineffective if you knew what you were doing." She turned to Esta. "I suppose you touched it?"

Esta bit her bottom lip and nodded. "Should I not have done so?"

"Obviously not if you hurt yourself, but I was more concerned about booby trap spells, or curses."

Esta laughed. "Oh, is that all? Rubbish!"

Katrine snorted. "You wouldn't laugh if you had seen the things I have. Promise me you'll be more careful. Call me first before you go touching anything even remotely suspicious."

"Goddess, how am I supposed to know what is suspicious? That thing looks like an ornamental metal rod." She studied the object in Katrine's hand. "What is it?"

Katrine studied the runes. "Hard to be sure but from the symbols I understand, this appears to be a key to something."

Esta pulled out the map from the pile of papers. She unfolded it and laid it on the desk. Katrine placed the rod beside the lettering on the map.

"It's the same language on chart and rod," Katrine said. "What do you make of the map? An island?"

Esta's heart had resumed its hurried beat. "Yes, unless I am much mistaken, this is a treasure map and that rod may be the key to the treasure."

* * *

Sam hunkered down under a canvas in his skiff in Costa harbor. It was uncomfortable but at least he was on his own and could think through the events of the last two hours. Somewhere out there, he had a mother, perhaps a whole family, just waiting to be discovered. His heart ached at the hurt in Harah's eyes as he'd explained his need to find the woman who had abandoned him.

But it had to be done if he was ever to find contentment. Lately he had felt restless, as though there might be more to life than pirating. Perhaps if he found his real family, they might provide a different existence. *Or they might tell you to take a long run off a short plank.* It didn't matter; he had to try at least.

He reached for the dagger in his boot as voices drifted over from the nearby dock. Two men conversed near his skiff. He strained his ears to pick up a clue as to their intention.

"I tell you, Lady M. plans to find this treasure. You and I could make a handsome profit, maybe retire somewhere safe with a warm woman."

"How do you know of it?" the second man asked, a thick edge of suspicion lacing his words.

"I keep my ears open, man. Do you want in or not? You supply the ship and I'll sort the crew - just small, mind, that's all we need."

Sam froze. Was it Lady Moonlight they were discussing? He pricked his ears at the idea of treasure but the thought of a certain woman made it difficult to lie still. He wanted to know more.

"Sure, I'm in," the suspicious man said. "Where do we sail for?"

"That's the beauty of it," the first man said. "Do you know the Pinnacle islands? Well, it's one of those. Not sure which yet but shouldn't be too hard to find. Just look out for the *Sea Sprite* and the rest will take care of itself."

He growled low in his throat. It was Lady Moonlight's ship alright, but she wouldn't be taking home the treasure this time. They had unfinished business. The men moved away but Sam lay planning his next adventure long into the night.

* * *

Esta stood on the captain's bridge behind, Lonso, who had been promoted to first mate after Stino's death.

"It's a perfect night for a treasure hunt, Lonso," she said, feeling more optimistic than she had in a long while.

"Sure is, Captain." Lonso's grin showed more gaps than teeth. "You going to share the loot with us when we find it?"

"Of course, I will," she said, patting his shoulder. As she turned away, she caught the eye of her new man, Ice, and thought again he must have been named after the pale blue of his irises. She shuddered involuntarily, but he had been vouched for by Lonso and that was good enough for her. None of her men were fine upstanding citizens but they were brave and loyal - that was all that mattered.

She moved to the bow and stood with the wind in her face, the black strands of her wig streaming behind her. It was chill but not wet and she reveled in the dance of her ship over the waves. *Sea Sprite* was one of the joys of her life; sailing one of her great loves. When she was on the ocean, she was free of earthly ties and a little of its wildness seeped into her, giving her strength for the trials of estate life. Lately, she had found it almost impossible to return to the estate without a nagging sense of dread.

"You seem almost happy tonight, Sister," Katrine said, joining her in the bow. Katrine was wildness personified, with a lithe body and long black hair that she rarely tied back. Not for her the wig, as she had less need for a full disguise, shunning public life as she did. She wore leather breeches, flowing black shirts and a broad black satin mask decorated with stars. Her piercing blue eyes were now fixed on Esta.

"I *am* happy, Katrine," she said. "What makes you think I'm ever unhappy?"

"I see the way you are," Katrine said, "and the way Mother treats you, like her own personal servant."

Esta frowned. "I love Mother."

"Of course, you do, but that doesn't mean you have no need for a life of your own. I've been out and seen things you'd never believe. You should spread your wings, before it's too late."

"And who would look after Mother and the estate?"

"We're not all as stupid and incompetent as you think," Katrine said. "Let go a little and you might be surprised." She turned and stalked away, boots clacking on the deck, long purple fingernails combing her hair in a familiar gesture from their childhood. Esta frowned. That was strange and out of the blue.

She couldn't imagine what had happened to bring on that conversation, but she would think on it. Perhaps her little sister was right, and it was time to think of herself for a change?

* * *

The Singing Pirate rode the bow of his ship, his looking glass trained on a speck in the distance. *Sea Sprite*. She was a tidy little ship, perfect for smuggling, with her small draught that could slip into shallow waters and out again with none the wiser.

It had taken him almost a day to track down the illusive Lady Moonlight. Even knowing where she was headed, he'd had no definite idea when she'd be casting off. Her ship's regular berth was a mystery, not that a smuggler would broadcast the headquarters of her business. An itch started at the base of his skull as he mused on the improbable career of this woman. He had to know more about her.

Another ship shadowed her, around the same size as *Sea Sprite* and far enough back that those on the leading vessel might not notice. But Sam had seen them and intended to keep a keen eye on the ship. His *Silver Lady* was a long way behind *Sea Sprite,* but he was confident they could catch up during the night hours when his *Lenweri* crew had the advantage of superior vision.

He startled as Nande, his second-in-command, appeared at his side. "Damn it, man. How many times have I told you not to sneak up on me?"

Nande frowned. "I am sorry, Captain. I forgot."

He huffed out a breath. He must be cranky to let the elf worry him. "What do you want?"

"I wished to advise that all was well with the ship and its course. We are holding a steady distance from *Sea Sprite* and the dawn should see us draw level with her. Will you board the vessel?" Nande's unblinking eyes gave no hint of his feelings on the matter.

"I haven't decided yet." Sam wasn't big on planning, preferring to stay flexible and let events dictate his plans. Some said that was foolhardy, but his elven crew accepted his way and were never perturbed. He admired that about them. "What do you think?"

Nande blinked. "You are asking me, Captain?"

"Yes, what would you do? Board the ship before they find the treasure or wait out of sight and claim it after the lady has done all the hard work of retrieving it?" He favored the second option.

"I believe there is too much uncertainty if we wait," Nande said. "I would advise seizing the ship at the earliest possible opportunity, restrain the crew and fetch the treasure yourself."

Sam nodded. He could see the wisdom in this plan but what if the lady harbored a secret about the treasure that she wouldn't share with him? No reason for her to help him steal her bounty. No, he still favored waiting.

"Thank you, Nande. I'd like you to catch up with *Sea Sprite* overnight, but don't let them know we're there. No noise and no lights. I want the advantage of surprise."

"As you wish, Captain," Nande said. "I will see to it."

The dark elf nodded and moved away silently in his soft leather shoes.

Sam turned back to the sea. The sun was setting, muting the colors of the ocean from glorious green to indigo blue. He loved this time of day when the wind had dropped, and peace settled over the sea. It was a balm for an otherwise turbulent life.

As they had often over the last few days, his thoughts turned to the recent revelations regarding his birth mother. What would happen if he found her? Would it help him to find a place in this world? Or would his mother reject him once more? Should he even bother with a woman who had turned her back on him over thirty years ago?

The clock couldn't be wound back, and he had no desire to complicate matters. Still, there was that nagging sense of loneliness and if he could relieve that, then perhaps finding his mother would be worth the risk.

CHAPTER 4

ESTA yawned and stretched her arms toward the dawn sky as she came on deck. A smile tugged at her lips and excitement zinged through her veins. It would be a brilliant day today and she'd find the treasure. Perhaps it might even be enough for her to stop smuggling and create a legitimate shipping business; be able to afford another vessel and crew and make her mark on the world. Her father would be so proud, just as he was when she proved she could sail this ship herself.

But dreaming of such things when she had not even found the treasure was foolhardy. She nodded to Lonso who gave her his customary gap-toothed grin. A couple of other sailors were on deck, checking the sails and lines, with one in the main top castle searching for their target island. They had narrowed down their search to two of the islands in this group and then ruled out one of these when they landed late yesterday afternoon. It had none of the landmarks the map had described.

"Land ahoy!" The lookout pointed to the southwest. Esta could just make out a small island through the mist that hung over the water. It would soon burn off and it looked as though they would have their bounty by the end of the day. If only that was the case!

"Raise more sail," she shouted, and extra hands leaped to do her bidding. The boat surged through the tranquil waters, cutting a path in the mist. The island loomed before them.

Esta's heart lurched and then galloped away, as a dark ship, similar in size to *Sea Sprite* materialized out of the mist on her starboard bow.

It was angling toward them and, if it continued its course, would cut them off. It couldn't be coincidence that the ship should appear when they were so close to their target!

"Lady Star!" she shouted. A call went up all over the ship for her sister.

Katrine appeared from below. "Yes, Sister?" Her smirk disappeared as she spied the other ship. "Who the hell is that?"

"Does it matter? Look at them! They're trying to cut us off from that island. Prepare to defend the ship."

Katrine turned and bolted to the gun deck, and then climbed the mizzen mast to the castle at its top. From there she could work her magic in relative safety and have a good view of the action below.

Esta turned to the crew who were waiting for orders. "Man the guns! Lonso, swing to port so our guns hit full on and keep her that way!"

She bounded up the stairs to the quarterdeck, the better to survey her crew. She stood and watched the ship approach. It was coming fast and still turning to port.

"Keep correcting, Lonso!" But the dark vessel had already driven them away from their destination. "Lady Star! Do your worst!"

A fireball sliced through the air above the ship and fell into the water short of the attacking vessel. Another followed and this one hit its target, burning its way through the main sail. More fireballs hit sails and rigging, setting all ablaze. The sailors on the dark ship were soon busy putting out fires, but the vessel came on, forcing them around and getting closer all the time.

"Fire!" Esta shouted, and her four guns on the starboard side boomed out. Only one hit, taking out the enemy ship's foremast; the rest flew too high. "Guns down!"

A low grinding echoed through *Sea Sprite's* deck as the cannons were moved lower. The seconds ticked by and her nerves wound tighter with each one. She opened her mouth to order the next shot but a huge blast from the enemy ship heralded the firing of their three port cannons.

"Incoming!" She threw herself on the deck grabbing hold of a rail to steady herself.

The ship shuddered beneath her and Esta trembled as though she had taken a blow to her own body.

Sea Sprite! She turned over onto her back frantically seeking her sister. Katrine was still aloft, casting fireball after fireball at the enemy ship. She was tiring, her magic barely strong enough for the fire to reach the ship. When it did it was easily extinguished.

Sea Sprite shuddered again heralding another cannon strike. Her guns were underwater, useless, and the dark ship had deployed rowboats full of black-garbed sailors. Esta struggled to her feet as the deck took a lurch to starboard. They were taking on water fast. She looked around, trying to count her crew. Several were missing.

Below decks?

She flew down from the gun deck and toward a hatch trying not to notice every heave and groan of her ship. She slipped through the hatch and slid down the ladder, landing in ankle deep water. Two men struggled toward her, both saturated, one with a bleeding forehead.

"Hold's full of water, Captain," Orto said. "Don't try to go down. I think we're all out." As the ship listed further to starboard Esta was flung against the bulkhead.

"I'll check the cabins." She continued along, opening door after door until she reached her own. She had to get the key and the map.

She opened her cabin door and Ice stepped through it into the passageway.

"This what you're after, Captain?" he asked, tucking the objects she sought into his shirt.

"Thank you, Ice." She reached for the precious items.

"I don't think so," he said, stepping to the side and grabbing her arm. He pushed her as the ship gave another lurch. She flew through the open door into her cabin and crashed into the chest beside her bed. A blinding pain seared her skull as the door slammed shut and her vision faded.

* * *

Sam prowled his gun deck like a caged lion. They were close to the action but not close enough. Just on dawn, the dark ship had made a beeline for *Sea Sprite* and, before he knew it, the two were engaged. The *Lenweri* had voted to leave them to it but Sam wasn't having a bar of that.

"Faster, Nande," he shouted. "More sail!"

The two ships had slowed as they engaged so it wasn't difficult to catch up. They hadn't even noticed the larger vessel looming to port.

Sam's mind worked hard as he considered the best way to tackle the situation. *Sea Sprite* was sinking. He didn't fancy getting caught up in the maelstrom when she went down. All the sails on the dark ship were damaged leaving her becalmed. He could sit back and wait for these two to sort it out, but if *Sea Sprite* went down, he might lose the tools he needed to find the treasure. And what of Lady Moonlight?

"We're going to board her," he shouted.

"Which one?" Nande asked.

"*Sea Sprite*." Yes, there was mutiny in those *Lenweri* eyes.

"She's sinking." No excitement or fear, just a flat admission of fact.

"She's also the key to the treasure. I want you to board *Sea Sprite* and secure her."

They weighed anchor, bow facing to the warring ships, leaving six *Lenweri* behind to guard the ship. Along with twenty-four elves, Sam launched the boats and rowed to the stricken vessel. She had listed so far to starboard the barnacles on her portside hull were visible.

"Board!" The rowboats were tethered to the ship with grappling hooks and the *Lenweri* scampered up the side of the ship, bows and quivers slung over their shoulders.

Sam had to use the lines to haul himself up and by the time he reached the rail his arms burned with the effort. He took a moment to process the scene.

Men battled back and forth across the tilted deck, both the lady's motley crew and opponents in black clothing. A man with pale blue eyes stood frozen near one of the hatches on the main deck, hands clutched to his chest. He appeared to struggle against an unseen force. Of Lady Moonlight there was no sign.

The *Lenweri* awaited his instruction.

"Black shirts are from *Storm Chaser*, the enemy ship," Sam said. "Do your best to disarm all fighters then group and guard them." The *Lenweri* moved forward subduing the winners of individual battles and pushing them into two groups according to ship of origin.

As Sam moved toward the frozen man, *Sea Sprite* creaked and settled further to starboard. It wouldn't be long now. He stopped before the man and searched him, pulling a map and rod from inside the crewman's shirt.

"Now then," Sam said, tucking the objects inside his own tunic, "where is the lady of this ship? Tell me and I might spare your life."

The man shook his head, teeth clamped in a grimace.

"He can't speak," said a feminine voice from behind.

Sam turned to find a dark-haired, masked woman with vibrant blue eyes. "Who are you?"

"You may call me Lady Star, pirate."

He stifled a groan at finding yet another vexatious woman onboard. "Why can't he speak?"

"I have him bound and gagged and thus he will stay. My sister is still below. Ice had her belongings, so I assume he knows where she is." She gave a flourish of her hand and the man's head snapped up.

"Witch! I'll see you hang for this!"

Sam's hand was around the man's throat in a second. He squeezed and the scum began to choke.

"Tell me where she is," he said, releasing the pressure a little.

"Her cabin." Ice coughed.

Sam bolted through the hatch and down the ladder, battling his way through shin deep water and pushing off from the bulkhead to keep himself upright. *Sea Sprite* shifted as water found its way into different compartments in the hold.

Finally, he reached the captain's cabin, placed his shoulder against the door and gave an almighty heave. Water rushed into the cabin with him as the ship's stern settled into the water. It cascaded over Lady Moonlight's prone figure.

He fell to his knees and crawled to her.

Is she dead?

Her pale face, blue lips and the nasty gash on her forehead seemed to indicate that fact. As the water flowed over her face she coughed, her eyelids fluttered, and her throat convulsed. He pulled her to him, out of the water that was still pouring into the cabin.

"Sorry, Lady." He lifted her over his shoulder and stood, her backside nestled against his cheek. "Not the most elegant way to be carried but necessary." He staggered from the cabin, pulling them through the door and up the sloping passageway by the door frames, before climbing the ladder to the hatch. He deposited Lady Moonlight into her sister's arms.

"See to her," he said, looking around the deck. The fighting was over and the men from *Storm Chaser* had gathered in the bow.

"*Sea Sprite*'s crew, listen up. This ship is about to sink. I can rescue you, but you need to swear to obey my orders. Do you agree?" He glanced down at the sister who looked daggers at him. He hoped she didn't choose this moment to demonstrate her magic.

A short discussion followed and then the first mate stepped up. "We agree, Captain."

Sam shoved Ice forward. "This man left your lady to die in her cabin. Take him and the crew of *Storm Chaser* in their ship to the nearest atoll and drop them there. You'll need to take some of *Sea Sprite*'s sail. When you've completed the task, bring *Storm Chaser* to me."

There was angry muttering from *Storm Chaser*'s crew.

"*Sea Sprite* men! Choose your best and strongest to help my *Lenweri* guard these men and sail the ship. You may take half the rowboats. The dead you will toss over the side."

"Ay, ay, Captain."

The men were soon sorted into their groups, under Nande's watchful eye. Sam turned back to the remaining sailors. "Abandon ship for my vessel and make it snappy."

"Yes, Captain."

"Wait a minute, pirate," the lady's sister said. "I'll not let you take over."

He raised one brow. "Lady, this ship is sinking and your sister needs help. Let's get her off this wreck and you can argue later. No doubt she will too."

"No doubt," she said.

They scrambled over the portside of the ship hot on the heels of those bound for *Storm Chaser*. Sam hoped the crew of *Storm Chaser* wouldn't give trouble, but he feared he'd given those guarding the group a difficult task.

Sam once again hauled Lady Moonlight up and over his shoulder. He went first, navigating the slippery portside of *Sea Sprite*, certain with each movement of the ship that he and the lady would tumble into the ocean.

Somehow, he managed to reach one of the row boats and slumped in the prow, the lady in his lap. He lay there, chest burning as he sucked in great gulping breaths, watching as the others followed, filling the rowboats beyond their safe capacity.

If they all made it back to *Silver Lady*, how was he ever going to get Lady Moonlight on board? *Stupid!* He was an idiot to even have contemplated plucking the woman from a sinking ship!

"This is charitable of you, pirate," Lady Star said. "I had no idea thieves had such good hearts."

"Humph," he said. "You and your sister are little better. What would you have me do? Sail on past?"

Her eyes narrowed. "I saw what you took from Ice. You're after the treasure. That's the only reason you stopped."

He looked down at the woman in his lap. "One of the reasons."

Lady Star laughed. "Do you mean you can't resist a damsel in distress?"

"What if I can't? You should be damned glad I came along."

* * *

Esta strode through the fog, her skull aching fit to burst. Why was there no damned light? There was something she should remember but it wouldn't come; it lurked in the corner of her mind, just out of sight. Gradually, she became aware of a light in the distance and moved toward it, the ache in her skull increasing with the glare.

Sea Sprite! Her ship was in trouble and she couldn't get to it.

She rocked and lay on something only a little soft. Voices argued around her. She opened her eyes and the strong mid-morning sun sent spikes of agony through her skull.

She moaned and closed her eyes, trying to sit up at the same time. A hand stopped her.

"Steady, Sister, you're in no condition to move yet. Besides, you'll capsize this boat."

She steeled herself for the pain and opened her eyes. "Let me sit up," she snapped. "The sun is killing me!"

Katrine helped her sit and Esta shaded her eyes. Her first sight was *Sea Sprite* sitting at an odd angle in the water and disappearing fast. "What are you doing? Lonso, for the sake of the Goddess, you should be below decks repairing the hole and pumping out the water."

Lonso flinched and averted his eyes. "No hope for her, Lady. It was her or us."

"Ridiculous," she snapped. "Truly, I'm ashamed to be your captain in moments like this. That ship is irreplaceable!"

"Actually, Moonlight, you're no longer captain of this crew," a familiar voice said.

She turned to find the Singing Pirate's green gaze upon her.

"You! I hoped never to see you again," she said, then turned to glare at Katrine. "You're as bad as these men, Lady Star. I thought I could trust you, and what happens when my back is turned?"

Katrine folded her arms across her breasts. "We had more on our mind than your stupid ship - like saving your life!"

"Go back," she said, turning to the pirate. "I assume you've taken command of my crew?"

"You assume correctly and you're being unfair, if I may say so. Your ship is doomed. You have to know when you're defeated, Lady."

She looked back at *Sea Sprite* and physical pain crushed her chest, making her forget her aching head. Becoming captain of the *Sprite* had been her proudest moment. She was free on the ocean, happy like she'd never been on land. Now, the Goddess had taken it from her. She'd never be able to afford a replacement. Her shoulders slumped as she envisaged what the death of her ship would truly mean for them all. She lowered her head to her hands and cried.

CHAPTER 5

WHEN Lady Moonlight crumbled, Sam didn't know what to do. He looked to Lady Star and she pulled her sister into her arms.

"There, there, Sister. This is a cruel blow but in time you'll prevail, and a new ship may be found for us to continue our trade. I'll do whatever I can to help. Let's board the pirate ship and recover from our trauma."

Lady Moonlight sniffed as she pulled out of her sister's arms. "This man would take everything from us. He can't be trusted."

"Still," the younger woman said, "we have few options at the moment."

"Don't forget I'm sitting right here," Sam said, dismayed at the way the lady could anger him.

She turned to him, flinching at the movement. "I know where you are, pirate, and I'm not ashamed for you to know exactly what I think of you!"

"I saved your life, you ungrateful woman!"

"Oh, and for that I'm supposed to thank you, even though you let my ship die?"

"You infuriating, miserable excuse for humanity," he said, incredulous that this woman could not spare a small shred of gratitude for the risk he'd taken. His shoulders and arms still ached from the effort of carrying her.

Lady Star chuckled and he glared at her. "What's so funny?"

"Yes," Lady Moonlight said. "I'd like to know that, too."

"Listen to yourselves." Lady Star looked from one to the other. "Doesn't it strike you as somewhat ridiculous that you're bickering like this when we've all just escaped death?"

He frowned at Lady Star. "Not in the least." He turned to her sister. "Does it seem ridiculous to you, Moonlight?"

"No! I don't appreciate you finding anything amusing in this, Sister."

At that, *Sea Sprite* gave a groan and slipped slowly below the water. Lady Moonlight lurched toward the edge of the boat as if to dive over and save her precious vessel. Sam gripped her shoulder, hoping to prevent her headlong dive over the side, and give her support. He regretted the loss. It was never easy to see a ship destroyed. He didn't know how he'd deal with the sinking of his own vessel. Except for the men rowing, they all sat watching the water swirl over the ship until all that was left was debris bobbing on the surface.

The rest of the trip passed in silence, the lady refusing to take her eyes from the place where *Sea Sprite* had disappeared. He was ill equipped for dealing with distraught women and the sister didn't seem to be able to break through Moonlight's melancholy either. When he embarked on this mission, he'd never dreamed catastrophe would force upon him the unwanted mantle of rescuer. But it had and now he had no earthly idea what he was supposed to do with the prickly woman and her motley crew.

They reached Sam's ship, and Lady Moonlight insisted on climbing to the deck without aid. He stayed below her to ensure she had help if she slipped and was rewarded with the sight of her shapely behind in black tights. Perhaps the aggravation would be worth it after all?

When he had taken care of the new sailors and seen their wounds were attended to, Sam looked for Lady Moonlight. He found her in the bow, sitting with her legs over the side, still gazing at the place where *Sea Sprite* sank.

He cleared his throat. "You should have that injury tended to, Moonlight. It could be serious."

She touched the wound below her hairline and flinched. "Needs stitches," she said. "My sister can do it when she's free."

"At least let me clean it for you and mix you a potion for the headache," he said, holding out the medicines he had brought over.

She glared at him. "What do you want, pirate? Half of everything I own is at the bottom of the ocean. What would you have of me?"

He pulled the map and metal rod from his shirt and her eyes widened. "I already have all I need. So you see, I could have let you drown with your ship."

"You have it!" She looked down at the water below as if trying to reason out her next move. Then she looked back at him. "What will you do with us?"

He smiled. "I have treasure to find, Lady. I intend to do just that. You'll stay with me as my guest until I'm successful and then I'll take you and your crew back to your home. Simple as that."

"That's my treasure!"

"I have the map and the rod which would seem to be some sort of key. You on the other hand have nothing, as you've so recently said. If you ask me, you should be glad to be alive."

Her fists bunched and her rich brown eyes turned flinty. "I found those, and I started this mission. I need that treasure, now more than ever. It might be enough to buy another ship or even mean I never had to smuggle again. I could just—"

Sam was intrigued. He was sure Moonlight had been about to say more than she should. He longed to know where she came from, expose the secrets that were so clearly a part of her world.

"I have my own crew and family to concern myself with," he said. "You should know all is fair among thieves, Moonlight, and thief you most certainly are, even though you hold yourself superior to me."

"I would never have done what you did. How did you find out about the treasure?"

"Same way the *Storm Chaser* captain did, I guess. Word on the street. Your man Ice was involved, I think."

Lady Moonlight drew in a sharp breath. "He is new!"

"Was, Lady. He'll be lucky to survive the day. I've dropped him and the remaining crew of *Storm Chaser* on an atoll. They'll be at each other's throats. It will be survival of the fittest."

The lady's eyes widened. "That's monstrous. No matter what they've done, you can't take the law into your own hands."

He drew himself up. "I can and I did. The law of the high seas is as I see fit. Those men attacked your ship. I doled out justice. Monstrous would have been to make them all walk the plank and take their chances with the sharks. How many would have survived then?"

"Still…"

"Still nothing!" His limited patience had run out. "Turn around, woman, and let me tend your face. If you remove your mask, it will make the chore easier."

The mask stayed in place, but in an odd way, it allowed Sam to appreciate the lady's features in isolation. Her eyes truly mirrored her soul. In their chocolate depths he discerned pain and hardship. They mesmerized him. Her lips were full and pink but seemed unaccustomed to smiling and certainly not kissing. As he gazed at them, he was drawn under her spell and had to pull away. Instead, he focused on the injury and gently dabbed the blood from the wound, then rested a cool square of cloth over it to ease the throbbing. She had her eyes closed now, her teeth biting into her bottom lip. Her forehead wrinkled and jaw clenched. It must hurt like hell.

"Here," he said. "I mixed a pain powder. My men swear by it." He held it out. She sniffed at it suspiciously, then drank it in one go.

Either she was beginning to trust him, or she felt so bad that death was a good option if it turned out to be poison. From the pallor of her skin, he decided it was the latter.

"You need to lie down." He stood and extended his hand. She gripped it, the calluses on her palm a reminder that she would not be easily dismissed. "You and Lady Star may take my cabin. She can stitch your wound there."

* * *

Esta was sick to her toes. Nothing could take her mind from the pull of needle and cotton through her forehead.

"This is deep," Katrine said, her serious eyes focused on the wound. "Do you have any double vision or feel like retching?"

"I had double vision when I awoke." She flinched as Katrine tugged the thread through. "There were two of that damned pirate. Surely one is enough?"

"We could have done with two of him back on *Sea Sprite*."

A shudder ran through Esta's body as she remembered the ship slipping below the water. "Would you mind not mentioning my ship?" she asked. "I can't deal with that right now."

"You'll have to face it sooner or later," Katrine said. "I lost everything too, you know. You don't see me weeping over it."

Esta glared up at her. "Do you think I care about my possessions? *Sea Sprite* was like an old friend to me. What will I do without her?"

"Purchase another one?"

"It won't be the same, even if we could afford it." She swore Katrine was less gentle than she had been. Surely it was not necessary to tug so on her skin. "Are you almost finished?"

"One more stitch," Katrine said. "If you ask me, you should be more grateful to the pirate. He risked his own life to save you. I didn't see anyone else lining up to go down and fetch you. And besides, he has the map and the key. It wouldn't hurt for you to butter him up. He might cut you a share of the loot."

"Are you suggesting I seduce the man?" She asked.

Katrine leaned closer to inspect her handiwork and gave the wound a last wipe. She fixed her bright blue gaze on Esta. "That's exactly what I'm suggesting. I've seen the way he looks at you. He's interested and he's not hard to look at. If I were you, I'd do all I could to ensure he kept me close."

"Well, it's fortunate I'm not you," Esta said. "Honestly, how can you suggest such a thing? I'm the high lady of house Aranati, not a whore who sells herself to the top bidder. I won't lower myself for anyone or anything."

Katrine shook her head. "And what do you call smuggling? You insist on telling me how poor we are and yet you stubbornly refuse any help."

"Whose help?"

"Mine for starters," Katrine said. "What I've suggested is perfectly sound advice and you've thrown it back in my face. Have some fun with this man. It won't hurt and it could help a great deal."

"You have fun with him if you're so fond of him."

Katrine's eyes narrowed. "I just might!" She walked to the door. "Get some rest. I'll have one of our men on guard outside." And with that, Katrine swept from the cabin, boots clicking on the polished floor.

She shook her head. What rubbish that girl spoke at times. And Katrine wondered why she never took her seriously!

* * *

While Lady Moonlight slept, Sam endeavored to bring order to *Silver Lady*. *Storm Chaser* returned with the *Lenweri* and the rest of *Sea Sprite*'s crew. He put Nande in charge of the new ship and gave him adequate crew to sail the vessel. He made Nande's aid, Landin, first mate on *Silver Lady* and asked him to see that everyone had somewhere to sleep and a job to do. It was crowded with the extra crew, but he didn't want the lady's sailors out of his sight.

Sam knew there would be friction between *Lenweri* and humans aboard his ships. He didn't even want to think about how awkward two captains on *Silver Lady* would be. Luckily the lady would have to take a step back. This was his ship and he was in charge. If she wanted to see her home, she'd have to accept his command. Besides, she was his prisoner.

Lady Star stalked up to him and he took a moment to admire the sway of her hips. She was not so captivating as her sister but still …

"How is she?" he asked.

"Suffering more than she'll admit to," Lady Star said. "It hasn't affected her stubbornness however." She folded her arms across her chest and let out a long breath.

"Listen, Lady," he said. "I wondered if, with more mouths to feed, you might be able to help in the galley."

Lady Star's eyes narrowed. "Oh, you did, did you? What do I look like, a serving girl? Find someone else to peel the spuds, pirate!"

With that, she stalked up to the main mast and began the climb to the top castle.

"Mm," he muttered. "That went well. I guess the answer is 'no'." He could have sworn he was captain around here. Looked like that didn't apply to the women.

*　*　*

When Esta went up on deck, she found the pirate captain studying the map - *her* map. She watched him, Katrine's words playing on her mind. He was handsome enough, but he was a pirate - no matter that she owed him her life, he had stolen from her and she must find a way to gain the upper hand. She looked up in the top castles and spied Katrine. Typical that her sister would isolate herself after their argument. They rarely saw eye to eye but suggesting she prostitute herself was going too far. Still…

She studied the captain, her head tilted to the side. It wouldn't hurt to be friendly. She could appear to be helpful and watch for a chance to seize the upper hand.

She wandered over. He stood as she approached and gave her a bow. She was surprised by his manners.

"Lady Moonlight," he said. "How are you feeling?"

"Like a coach has run over my head." She touched the stitches near her hairline.

"You're lucky it wasn't worse. Please sit. I have questions for you."

He waited until she was comfortable and then sat beside her.

"You've narrowed the search to the island just ahead of us?" he asked.

She quirked an eyebrow. "Certainly. It's the right shape and has the same features. I'm almost certain this is the island I seek."

"Almost?"

"One can never be sure, Captain. What's your name? I can't call you 'captain' forever."

He shrugged. "Most do."

"Is it a secret?"

"I don't throw my name about." He paused, frowning. "I don't know *your* real name."

"And you won't," she said. "However, I'd like to have a name to call you."

He looked down at his hands. "Delacost," he said. "Samael Delacost."

"Do the *Lenweri* know your name?"

"They do but I trust them implicitly."

"Why did you decide to trust me?" she asked.

"So many questions this afternoon, Moonlight," Delacost said, looking back at the map. "We're on the wrong side of the island. It appears there's a small river that allows access to the interior of the island. *Silver Lady* has a shallow hull, ideal for traversing small rivers. I think we should make our way around to the other side, enter the river and weigh anchor. *Storm Chaser* can follow us and remain at the mouth of the river as a guard. I'll leave some of your men with her."

She raised her chin. "It's a fair plan."

"We'll have a celebration tonight and set off in the morning in search of the treasure," he said, studying her. "You seem to have accepted your fate."

"I'm trying to make the best of a bad situation, Delacost."

"I hope that's all you're trying to do. I warn you, if you defy me, you'll be sorry." He stood and walked down the deck. Esta watched as he tucked the map back in his shirt.

"I'll defeat you if it's the last thing I do, Samael Delacost," she said to herself.

CHAPTER 6

THE mood was buoyant on *Silver Lady* that evening but Esta couldn't share in the happiness. She may be safe and well with a full belly but her future and those she loved was tied up with *Sea Sprite*. The pirate would have to forgive her if she appeared less than joyful. She sat on a thick coil of line and watched Katrine dance with Samael. He moved mighty well and, when he smiled, her stomach squirmed like a giant electric eel. If that look was directed at her, she'd have difficulty breathing let alone dancing. The knock to her head must've done more damage than she'd thought. It wasn't like her to lose her head over a man.

Katrine on the other hand seemed immune. She swayed her hips and stamped her feet but was her usual aloof self. Esta had never seen Katrine take interest in any man. Perhaps she was one to fancy women? Then again witches were bound to have strange fetishes. Esta studied Delacost, struck once more by a nagging familiarity when his face turned to the light.

The dance ended and Katrine moved off toward the bow. Delacost picked up his lute and sat beside Esta, his thigh pressed against hers. Her heart danced a fancy rhythm, but she clawed her feelings back under control. There was no point allowing herself to be swept away by his handsome face and devilish attitude. Far better she should put her mind to the future and how to make ends meet without a ship.

He strummed a few bars on the lute and she was surprised at his skill.

"Father played the lute," she said, "but I never learned. I still remember the nights we gathered after dinner to sing. He had a wonderful voice."

Samael began humming along with the notes. She remembered the tune and opened her mouth. The song poured from her, taking her back to her childhood. When the last note died, her cheeks were wet.

Samael offered her a handkerchief. It was crisp and white, hardly what she would've expected from a pirate. She sniffed. "Thank you."

"You have a beautiful voice too, Moonlight," he said. "Is your father dead?"

The question hurt. "There isn't a day goes by that I don't miss him." She gazed up at the stars and the clouds that raced across them. "Are your parents alive?"

She looked over at him in time to see a tortured look flit across his face. It was gone in a moment and she decided she'd been mistaken.

"My parents are very much still with me though I don't see them often. It's difficult in my profession."

"Clandestine meetings with them, I imagine." She dried her eyes and blew her nose, breathing in the spicy scent of the cloth. Her heart thumped again. "They must miss you."

"Mother especially," he said. "She has no other children. Most of the time they don't know if I'm alive or dead."

"That would be truly awful."

He frowned and fell into a brooding silence.

"You play well," she said. "Please, play a happy tune?"

He roused himself and began a merry sea shanty that had Esta clapping along and Lonso pulling Katrine up for a dance.

By the time Samael stopped playing, she knew it was time for sleep. The music was bittersweet; the joyful notes reminding her she had no reason to be happy. Her head had begun to pound in time with the deck-stomping sailors. Her vision blurred and she closed her eyes.

As she nodded off, strong arms lifted her, and she was enveloped in Samael's unique scent. She was immediately wide awake, panic surging through her. His simple touch had so much power over her - too much.

"I can walk," she said, kicking her feet around.

He lowered her slowly, and the brush of his body against hers did nothing to calm her racing pulse. He kept his arm around her as her feet touched the deck. As her traitorous body sagged against him for support, her common sense bade her take a step away. She fussed with her tunic so she wouldn't have to look into his eyes. When she did finally meet his gaze, its intensity stole her breath. Her head began to spin, and she staggered to the side. He was there again, both arms enfolding her in a manner that was too intimate. *I can't get away from him!* She stiffened and pushed at him, trying to locate Katrine.

"Lady Star!" she said, hating the distress which laced her words. Hating to admit she needed her sister.

Katrine appeared, took one look and guided Esta toward the hatch. "I can manage from here, Captain," she said.

It seemed a long walk to their quarters. Katrine kept up a soothing monologue and her voice lulled Esta's distress. Once in the cabin, her sister removed her boots and put her to bed. Her last thought was the hope she would wake on the morrow and find this day had been but a bad dream.

* * *

Sam found an old bed roll and made his rest in the bow of the ship. It was cool but the inky black sky, broken by thousands of stars and a yellow crescent moon, soothed him. The celestial bodies seemed like old friends who had guided him his entire life.

As he watched the clouds scoot across the sky, he mused on the prickly woman who was his guest.

She had displayed a fragile beauty under the moonlight this evening. He had seen a softer side, far more tender than her sister. He suspected she had grown a tough shell over the years as protection. It was clear she was used to fending for herself as well as those under her care; she didn't appreciate being vulnerable.

But vulnerable she was, and he sensed she was so even before her ship went down. Something told him the beautiful lady had been walking on the edge of a precipice for some time and not only financially. It was none of his business, of course. She was naught to do with him. He mistrusted the way his heart wanted to shield her. Since when could he protect a woman? He was a pirate and a pirate he'd stay. The sooner he found the treasure and set himself free of this woman, the better.

CHAPTER 7

ESTA glared at Katrine's back as they hacked their way through the dense bush of the island. Following the map had led them up a narrow river to a waterfall and they had weighed anchor at the base of the falls. It was an idyllic spot if she had been able to appreciate it. The falls threw up a fine mist and the area was sheltered from wind. Bird calls echoed and an exotic perfume hung on the air. If only she could find the origin of that fragrance, she'd make a fortune back in the cities of the kingdom.

Samael had ordered half her crew to remain with the ship, along with half of the *Lenweri*.

He's fond of half measures, that one.

But the reason for the glare directed to her sister was the difficulty of the terrain and the ease with which Katrine sliced her way through the persistent branches that sprang into their path. It had to be her magic and simply wasn't fair.

They followed a game trail beside a creek that trickled down from the hills above. The map showed their destination as the crest of one of those hills - the tallest, of course. Samael led the group with a handful of the strongest *Lenweri* to blaze the trail and clear the brush. Then came herself and Katrine, her sailors and another handful of *Lenweri*. Esta had not had much to do with the elves but had heard the kingdom was under threat from them. She wondered what part these elves had to play in the unrest in the kingdom. Samael appeared to enjoy their company and she couldn't fault their competence at tasks, but they avoided her. Perhaps he had asked them to stay away?

They were nearly halfway to their destination when they stopped for luncheon. She collapsed on the ground beside the stream and splashed water on her face then took a long drink. The taste was glorious after the stale cask water they'd been consuming. Most of the time she preferred to drink watered wine.

Samael stopped beside her. "How do you fare, ladies? Coping?"

"Yes, Captain," Katrine snapped.

"Some of us are doing it tougher than others," Esta said, glaring at Katrine.

Her sister looked down her nose. "Just using the gifts at my disposal."

Esta didn't like the smirk on Samael's face. "I'm the one who nearly died yesterday, and you insisted I come on this trek, Captain."

His mouth dropped open. "I insisted? I asked you to remain behind as I suspected how tough this would be. It was *you* who insisted on coming, though I don't know why when it no longer has anything to do with you."

She frowned so hard that he stepped back. "Perhaps I still hope you'll change your mind and give me the treasure. It's the right thing to do."

His eyes turned cold. "I told you I wasn't concerned with what you thought was right. This treasure is *mine* by virtue of the fact that I vanquished your foe and saved your life. If you had any nobility, you'd see that!"

She froze. *Does he know about my title?* Was the use of the word nobility an accident or had he worked out who she really was? "We'll have to agree to disagree on that, Captain. If you were a chivalrous man you would have saved me and expected nothing but gratitude."

"And I would still have been disappointed!"

"Would you both stop this bickering?" Katrine had taken off her boots and was massaging her feet. "Honestly, you make my ears ache."

Esta snapped her mouth shut to quell the retort that hovered on her lips. Katrine was right. She was spending too much time fighting.

It would do no good antagonizing her rival. She would sit back and await her chance to seize the advantage.

* * *

Sam broke through a particularly dense patch of undergrowth and found himself on the rim of a huge grassy bowl. The sun was setting over the far side of the basin. He squinted against the glare, trying to make out the landmarks on the other side. Excitement prickled his scalp. The grassy bowl fit with the topography marked on the map. This could really be the right place. If it was, there would be a crack or crevice on the western side that led into a cave and the resting place of the prize.

Lady Moonlight came up behind him. Her perfume engulfed him, adding to this strange awareness he had for her. He clenched his stomach against it and tried to ignore her proximity.

"It fits the map," she said into the silence. "Almost exactly."

"Light torches," he said. "We're going down."

"Now?" Esta asked.

So much for ignoring her!

"Yes, now." He moved around, collecting dry sticks and larger firewood. "If you wish to be useful you can collect more wood while I get this started."

"Shouldn't we make camp and tackle this in the morning? It will be dark soon and dangerous."

"Stay here if you wish but I'm going down. That treasure has lain there long enough."

Lady Moonlight frowned. He was intrigued to know what was going through her mind. Was she hoping to delay him so she could sneak down with her men and spirit the treasure away? She hadn't a hope of doing that. If she got past him and the *Lenweri* here, she had another lot to face back at the ship. Perhaps the lady hoped to find the treasure and take a sample for herself. No, none of that was possible, even in her stubborn mind. He shook his head, sick of trying to second guess her.

"Wherever you go, I too shall go," she said. "Be it on your head if one of us falls in the dark."

"The *Lenweri* will see us safely down as long as they don't allow the torches to destroy their night vision. You're welcome to come, unless you're too tired, of course."

She pulled her shoulders back and raised her chin. "I could walk all night, Captain."

He couldn't help the chuckle that escaped. Walk all night indeed! She was dead on her feet and, truth be known, should be having an early night after yesterday's head injury. But he'd not be the one to tell her.

* * *

Esta's frustration simmered. They had spent all day hacking their way up this mountain only to have to forge a way down this animal trail. Katrine again worked in front, her boundless energy getting under Esta's skin as usual. They spent the entire night in the descent and, as the eastern sky lightened behind them, she stepped from the track and collapsed on the grassy floor of the bowl.

She lay on her back in the damp grass, staring up at the sky, vaguely wondering if she would ever move again. Her head throbbed, her feet ached and the bandage around her forehead was wet with sweat and blood. She had scratches on every exposed piece of skin and a myriad of bites from the midges that had assailed them during the hours of dark. Samael approached and nudged her with a toe. She turned to him, ready to snap his head off but instead, was distracted by the sight of his chest gleaming in the faint light of dawn. He had loosened his buttons and was mopping his face and chest with his bandanna.

"You did well, ladies," he said. "That was as hard a trek as I've ever been on." His eyes ran down her body and her face heated.

He cleared his throat. "I thought we'd rest here for several hours, then tackle the crossing after a late breakfast."

Esta didn't wish to agree but she couldn't move another muscle if her life depended on it. "That would be welcome," she said.

Her black wig itched like the devil. She would've given anything to remove it right now. He watched her, seeming lost in thought.

"If you don't mind, Captain," she said. "I'll get some sleep while I can."

She sat up and began laying out her bedroll. By the time she had finished, Samael had moved to the far side of the camp and was making a fire. She fell asleep next to her sister, dreaming of a long hot bath and a decadent scalp massage.

* * *

Sam stood before a crevice in the rock face on the western side of the bowl. The location fit the map - this had to be the opening to the vault that held the treasure. He lit another brand in the fire and stepped toward the dark cleft. A hand reached out and grabbed his arm.

"Wait," Lady Moonlight said, staring fixedly at the fissure.

"What is it now?" he asked. "Do you wish to argue more about who wins and who loses out of this?"

She sent him a withering look. "When we found the map and key, there was a spell cast over them. This place could be guarded by one as well. If not here, then there may be one further in."

He turned back to the opening and swallowed his fear. He didn't like magic of any kind, although Lady Star made it seem rather entrancing. "Lucky we have your sister to investigate for us. Lady Star?"

The woman in question stepped up beside him. "I see no reason to help you when you've said you won't include us in the spoils. Unless you've changed your mind?"

He huffed out a breath.

Of all the manipulative, rotten…

He should just barge in and hang the risk but that would be stupid. Still, there may be no threat and then he would have handed part of the treasure to the women for no reason. It wasn't right! He'd earned this.

"Well, Captain?" Lady Moonlight said. "My sister has a point, don't you think? Or would you like to risk death by entering without her help?"

He looked to the heavens. "What did I ever do to deserve the company of two conniving women?"

Lady Star smirked but her older sister merely stared at him, arms crossed and awaiting his decision.

"Fine," he said. "Lady Star, would you be so kind as to check for spells before we enter. I'll cut you and Moonlight a share of the booty, say ten per cent?"

"Say fifty per cent and we have a deal," Lady Moonlight said.

"You leave me speechless, woman," he snapped. "This is what you planned when you insisted on coming, only I didn't see it until it was too late."

"Believe what you will," Lady Moonlight said. "It doesn't change the fact that you need us."

Sam ground his teeth, refusing to look at her and desperately seeking a way not to give in. There was none he could see.

"Deal," he said. "Fifty per cent share but only if you discern and disable at least one magic trap." That condition was pure genius.

Lady Moonlight didn't even consult her sister but nodded slowly. Boy, she was arrogant - totally unilateral in her approach to situations. By the look on her sister's face, it hadn't gone unnoticed.

He nodded back. "Good. Now, Lady Star can you work your magic so we can progress?"

Lady Star stepped toward the crevice. Eyes closed and palms outstretched. She advanced slowly until her hands touched the rock. Not a thing happened that he could see. She opened her eyes and muttered words that made no sense. Still nothing…

"Let me go first." She walked through the crevice and disappeared into the dark. When Lady Moonlight tried to follow her, he held her back.

"Wait," he said, every nerve in his body screaming at him to follow the young witch to ensure she was safe.

"Take your hands from me, Captain," Lady Moonlight snapped. "I don't need your protection or whatever it is you're trying to do."

"It wouldn't hurt you to let someone close once in a while, Lady." he said, refusing to remove his hands. The brown eyes that peered up at him were fearful.

Of him? "Do you trust anyone?" he asked.

She snorted. "Trust? How could I trust you? You robbed me of the keys to this treasure."

"Why must it always come back to that? You're alive because of me. Surely that has earned me a measure of trust?"

The look she sent him was even more wary. "Why do you care? After this, our paths need never cross."

"I don't know." It was a fair question. He shouldn't care but he did. It hurt him that she wouldn't allow him closer. He didn't even know her real name. "Perhaps I think it sad that you don't even trust your sister?" If he had a sibling, Sam didn't think he would disregard then as easily as this lady did her sister.

"I do trust her."

He raised his brows. "Do you?"

She turned away. "Of course, I do."

At that moment, they were saved by Lady Star's return. "It's safe for now. I detected no spells."

Sam smiled at her. "You could've told me you thwarted a dozen spells and how could I have proven you didn't?"

Lady Star tilted her head to one side. "I don't lie, Captain. My sister on the other hand…let's just say you're fortunate I'm the one with the magic." She turned and slipped back inside before Lady Moonlight had a chance to respond.

"Well?" he said.

"I do *not* lie," the lady snapped.

"Seems to support the lack of trust theory I proposed earlier." He lit a brand and passed it to her.

"Oh, shut up," she said, following Katrine through the fissure.

* * *

Esta entered a narrow slit through the solid rock of the hill. Katrine was just ahead, her torch bobbing in darkness that seemed to eat up the light. Samael grumbled behind her - something about foolhardy women. There was no room for him to squeeze past and take the lead, so he'd have to stay where he was. A handful of *Lenweri* brought up the rear, the remaining force from the *Silver Lady* having been left behind to guard the entrance.

He was wrong. She could and did trust. Didn't she? His words ate at her, challenged her. His very presence was an assault on her independence. When he was near, she found her ears tuning to him, her eyes drawn to him, her body urging a closeness that didn't make sense.

She knew little of him except he was handsome and brave and loved his parents. He appeared to be a good captain who looked after his crew. Was he a man worthy of her trust? More integral, was his earlier question - did she actually trust anyone? Katrine? When it came down to naming names, who made that list?

Esta was shocked to find she couldn't place anyone on that page. So shocked, she stopped dead in the passageway. Samael bumped into her. His hands reached out to prevent her fall - warm hands, capable hands, attached to strong arms that enfolded her waist and pulled her back against his chest. A tingle ran through her and she rested for a moment in the circle of his embrace, wondering what it would be like to be cared for by him.

"This is hardly the place for a romantic interlude, Moonlight," he whispered in her ear.

She was so stunned she couldn't speak for a time. "That's the furthest thing from my mind I assure you, Captain." She pushed away and his hands slid from her hips ever so slowly, almost a caress. She shivered, her thoughts conjuring his hands in other places on her body. She sensed he was gifted in the art of pleasuring a woman, while she was a complete novice. Excitement bubbled through her and she knew an aching regret as his fingertips slipped away.

Get a grip on yourself you ninny!

Years of denying herself the company of men must be catching up with her. Now of all times, she could hardly afford to be distracted by Samael Delacost's striking face and wandering hands.

They resumed their trek. Katrine's torch had disappeared but Esta discerned a lightening of the passage. That was surely impossible. She hurried forward, concerned for her sister and what she might find up ahead.

The passage opened out into a circular chamber. In the center was a huge stalactite balanced over a small pond. Sunlight streamed down through a fissure in the roof. Light struck the stalactite and radiated in all directions. Katrine stood gazing at it and Esta hurried to her side.

"I was worried for you," she said.

Katrine smirked. "I can look after myself."

Again, she was struck by the edge to Katrine's voice, as if something ate at her. Esta wished she would just say what was wrong, not jab and niggle. She didn't have time for games.

Delacost joined them. "Beautiful," he said. "That can't be ice, it's not cold enough. Is it crystal?"

"Yes," Katrine said. "I believe so. It's the site of the treasure. Now hush so I can determine how to defeat it."

"It's guarded then?" Samael asked, sending a look at the *Lenweri* that made them spread out through the chamber.

"I'll let you know if you give me some space."

He moved away from the edge of the pool and stood beside Esta, close enough for her to feel the heat coming from his body. His hand brushed hers and she jumped. It was just a chance touch but the charge that surged between them was real, not imagined. He looked down at her, excitement blazing from his eyes. A smile quirked his lips and she was drawn toward them. A shiver ran through her as she fantasized about those lips on her skin. His pupils dilated, eyes dipping toward her mouth. She swallowed several times but found no voice. Finally, she took a step away. The only way to deny this man was to stay remote, both physically and emotionally. He could never be anything but a nuisance. She had to remember that.

Instead, she focused on Katrine, taking a deep breath and wrapping herself in calm. She wasn't very good at calm. Little frissons of fear tripped around her body and she didn't know if it was the crystal or the man beside her firing her nerve endings.

Katrine appeared to be in a trance, her hands outstretched. The crystal began to pulsate, sending waves of blinding light into the chamber. Esta raised her hands to shield her eyes but even so, her skull throbbed in time with the light.

"Lady, are you well?" Samael took a step toward Katrine.

Esta pulled him back, the muscles of his forearm firm beneath her fingers. "If you interrupt, you could endanger my sister or yourself."

He looked down at her. "You do trust her then?"

"It seems in some things, yes I do. This is her area of expertise and she is good, very good."

"It's a strange trade to get into," he said.

"Hush."

She stared with rapt attention as the pulsations of the crystal increased in frequency, and then closed her eyes when she could no longer look upon the gem. She could see the flashes of the rock through her eyelids and her skull ached, but she could feel nothing else. She'd give anything to be able to do what Katrine could.

A cry rang through the chamber and she opened her eyes to find the crystal's light had engulfed Katrine. The two pulsed in ever frantic beats. She was no longer certain her sister could handle the magic contained within this space.

Esta hurried to her side. "What can I do?" she asked, squinting at the light.

Katrine's face was contorted with the strain of the battle she fought. *Is she losing the fight?* "Katrine, what can I do to help?" Her voice was low, urgent but free of the panic she struggled to control.

"Take Delacost…stand on the other side…hold hands and I'll direct part of the flow into you. You may be able to diffuse it."

Esta turned, grabbed Samael by the hand and pulled him around to the ledge opposite Katrine. The crystal hung between them. "Ready."

"Ready for what?" His hold was tight on her fingers. "Is she in trouble?"

"She is, Captain. Are you willing to take some of the light so she may win through?"

"Of course. Is it safe?"

She liked the way he immediately agreed before asking about the risk. "I don't know. I don't like what it's doing to her."

They had no more time to talk as they were engulfed in a blinding beam of light. It speared through Esta and it was as if another heart beat within. She gritted her teeth, took a deep breath and tried to welcome as much as she could into her body. Her joints ached, her toes curled in her boots and her hair stood on end. She had nothing to spare for Samael, all of her focused on handling the light within.

As suddenly as it came, the light winked out. She sagged as it left her and leaned, sobbing, against Samael. He took ragged breaths into his body and seemed not to be aware of her. Eventually his arms wrapped around her and she breathed in his spicy scent. Surprisingly, it calmed her.

When she raised her head, he was looking down at her, fear in his eyes. "I think we nearly died, Moonlight. Remind me of that the next time you drag me into the fray."

With his words, they both looked for Katrine. She had collapsed on the far side of the pond. Esta's fear took her breath as she ran around the rim to her prone sister. Her hands flew to Katrine's chest. She felt a steady heartbeat and collapsed across her sister, relief that she was alive overwhelming everything else.

"Is she…?" Samael asked.

"She's alive," Esta said, her face wet with tears.

"She won't be so for long if you squash her chest," he said. "Sit up so I can check her breathing."

She pushed up, embarrassed and berating herself for her stupidity. He was right, damn it. Katrine might not be out of the woods yet. She watched as Samael examined her sister, checking her breathing and feeling over her for hurts.

"She's breathing on her own but it's shallow," he said. "Her heart is strong enough and the only wounds I can find are these two small marks on her palms." He showed her the burns, at least that was what they looked like.

Esta removed her cloak, folded it and lay it under Katrine's head. She took her sister's hand. It was cold, except for the area of the mark which was still too hot to touch. "What can we do for her?"

One of the *Lenweri* stepped forward. "I might be able to help. My family are healers and our people understand magic."

She didn't hesitate. "Please, do what you can."

The elf laid one of his hands on Katrine's forehead and the other on her chest and closed his eyes. Esta's own chest hurt as she waited for his verdict. Finally, he opened his eyes. "I think she will be well. Only rest is needed."

"But you can't be sure?" She couldn't lose Katrine.

"Nothing in this life is certain, Lady." He looked at the pond. "Have you noticed the water is gone?"

She looked toward the pool and found it dry. An object in the bottom reflected the sun's rays. "Captain?"

He stood and crossed to the edge of the pond, jumping down into the dry bottom. He stooped to collect the object. "A lady's earring." He pulled something from his shirt.

The metal rod! Her heart picked up its pace as Samael leaned under the crystal. A grinding ensued and she released Katrine's hand and stood. A circular platform, a pace in diameter, rose from the center of the pond's base. As far as she could see, it was empty.

CHAPTER 8

SAM squatted beside the platform - the empty platform. All they had been through to get here rolled through his mind and now it seemed a cruel trick. Or someone had beaten them here. He stood and turned to Lady Moonlight, the earring clasped in one fist. He made his way back to the side and climbed up.

"It's empty?" she asked.

"There's only this." He held out the earring. It was unique; a gold setting with a vibrant opal that caught the light and radiated multi-colored magnificence.

"It's beautiful," she said, her voice hushed.

"Not much use as a single earring," he said. "Though I could get my ear pierced and rename myself the opal pirate."

Moonlight glared at him. "You *would* think it was yours to keep."

Lady Star groaned and her sister flew to her side. "Sister, are you well?"

"Where am I and why is my bed so damned hard?" Lady Star pushed her hand through her hair. "Ouch!" She peered at her palm. "Why is my hand burned?"

"It was the effect of the light," he said. "Both palms."

She groaned again. "Everything aches, my chest hurts, my eyes feel like they are boiling in their sockets. She looked up and he gasped. Her eyes were brilliant chips of blue fire instead of their usual sapphire.

"What's wrong?" she asked.

He looked at Lady Moonlight hoping she'd take the lead, but she stared at her sister, eyes wide. He turned back to the witch. "Can you see?"

"Of course, I can see," she snapped. "Just tell me what's wrong."

"Your eyes," he said, "They're changed, brighter, blinding."

"Rubbish!" She put her hand before her eyes. Her palm showed the glittering reflection of her orbs. "No, no, no," she moaned. "This can't be happening. I can't function if everywhere I go, I scare people."

The *Lenweri* cleared his throat. "If I may say something?"

"Go ahead, Ethron," Sam said.

"I have heard of this before - the eyes. They fade but their brilliance will remain enhanced. You will be noticed but not so much as now."

Lady Star stared at him. "You can't know that." She looked from Esta to Sam. "Where's the treasure?"

He again looked to Moonlight, but she frowned back. "Lady Star, after the crystal went quiet, we saw the water had drained from the pond. I used the key and a platform rose. All that was left was this." He lifted the single earring. "It should be yours," he said, handing the opal over.

"Gone," she said. "All for naught." She lifted the earring to her left ear lobe and pushed the hook through the flesh. A drop of blood gathered on the skin she had just pierced. The stunning opal hung, reflecting the light, a fitting accompaniment to the lady's eyes.

He flinched at the thought of piercing his own ear. Lady Star was one unusual woman. He turned to Moonlight, wondering if she was as discomforted by the display as he was. By the pallor of her skin, she was.

"Let's get out of this place." Lady Star climbed to her feet and strode from the chamber.

CHAPTER 9

FOUR long weeks after her adventure in the crystal cavern, Esta and her maid alighted from the coach in the forecourt of Wildecoast Castle. She was wondering where her aunt was when the aging seamstress bustled down the stairs.

"Esta, Esta," she said, placing a kiss on each cheek and pulling her niece into a hug. "I've so looked forward to this. Your dress is ready. You won't believe how beautiful it is. The queen herself will be envious."

Esta smiled at the torrent of words. Aunt Paurella was the Queen's Dressmaker and full of the love of life. She never failed to lift her spirits. Pair that with the queen's ball this evening and she had begun to believe she might shake off the gloom that had enveloped her over the last three weeks; the time that had elapsed since Samael had put them ashore near the river on the edge of her estate.

"Come, come, my girl," Paurella said. "It has been a long trip. You'll want refreshments."

Esta ordered her maid and footman to bring her luggage and followed her aunt, who kept up a constant stream of words on palace gossip and the goings on in the kingdom.

"I've had you placed in a suite two doors from mine. Your maid has a small room in there as well. But come to my chambers and we'll have afternoon tea. Do you wish to use the palace baths? No? Then I'll have a bath prepared in your room."

She had forgotten how many words streamed from Paurella's mouth. She smiled and let the deluge wash over her. At least there wasn't a need to say much and that suited her very well.

They entered her aunt's chambers and there, on a dressmaker's mannequin, was one of the most gorgeous gowns she could ever have imagined. It was a deep emerald green satin, with small puffed sleeves dropped provocatively off the shoulder. A full skirt, with a flounce at the back, flowed into an emerald lace train. She imagined the dress would expose a daring amount of bosom. But it was exquisite.

"Is this mine?" she asked, hardly daring to believe it could be so.

"That it is, Esta," Paurella said. "And I'll hear no nonsense about you not being worthy. You work jolly hard. I want you to let your hair down tonight. Dance with a handsome man." She handed Esta an elegant silver mask edged with green lace. "Everyone will be masked tonight, and I imagine that will free inhibitions."

She fixed the mask in place and looked at herself in the mirror. "Perhaps I *will* let my hair down at that," she said, but she found the prospect of dancing with a stranger in a mask unnerving.

All the fun in the world wouldn't solve any of her problems. Instead of enjoying herself, perhaps her efforts would be better spent in gaining financial help for her estate. A fling with an attractive man would achieve little unless he was also wealthy.

The afternoon passed in a whirlwind of bathing, perfuming, hair teasing and make up. Esta was now ready to brave the ball. At least she told herself she was ready. In actual fact, she was more nervous than usual. Could she carry off this dress or would the upper nobility know she was a fraud; that she somehow didn't deserve to wear this gown or dance in this company?

As she stood before the long mirror in her room, she was thrilled at the way the gown hugged her curves and showed off her shoulders and bosom to their best advantage. She stepped into her silver slippers and settled the beautiful mask over her features. Her chestnut hair was artfully arranged on top of her head with wispy tendrils escaping from the sides and back. The queen had loaned her an emerald necklace and earrings to complete the look, though how Aunt Paurella had persuaded the monarch to do such a thing, she couldn't imagine.

She took one last look and turned as her aunt entered.

"You're gorgeous, Esta. I hope you have a magical night."

Esta would be happy if no magic were involved. She had developed an aversion to it since that day in the crystal chamber. "Thank you, Aunt Paurella. This dress and all you've done for me is a treasure beyond words."

"I want you to be happy. You deserve it."

She smiled and hugged her aunt before stepping into the hall where a page waited to escort her downstairs.

There were no announcements that evening since it was a masquerade ball. She hated being announced, having every eye upon her, so she was glad to be able to glide up to the doorway of the ballroom in silence. Her escort bowed and scurried away as she turned to survey the room.

There were already many in attendance though she couldn't see the royal couple. She spied Lord Nikolas Cosara, admiral of the King's Navy, and his new wife, Lady Merielle. Merielle's red hair stood out like a beacon. There was much speculation around Merielle and where she had come from but Esta didn't care. Everyone had secrets, things they didn't wish to share. She liked Merielle and wished she had the time to get to know her better.

Esta stepped through the doorway and began to make her way across to the Cosaras, but was stopped by a man in a blue velvet jacket and black velvet pants. It had to be Lord Tomas Hen who swept her into a dance, since he loved velvets. It was pleasant enough. She was encouraged by the warm look in his caramel eyes, but this was hardly the handsome man she sought. If she was even seeking such! There was no point taking on her aunt's wild ideas. Tonight may be enjoyable, but the thought of a wild liaison, that she would regret in the morning, turned her stomach to ice.

After the dance, she excused herself and continued toward Nikolas and Merielle, who now chatted with another couple. She would swear it was Kain Jazara, once army general, and his wife Lady Alique Zorba. The sight of them holding hands sent a pang through her.

What's wrong with me? I've never been so soppy sentimental before! Since the treasure hunt, her emotions were uncertain; one minute, strong and resilient, and the next a shaking mess. She blamed the experience in the crystal chamber. Katrine, too, was a changed woman and had left the estate in search of answers to her new condition.

Before she could reach the two couples, another masked man asked her to dance. She spent the next hour being whirled around the dance floor on one or another man's arm. It was exceptional fun except for when a fat lord stood on her foot and pinched her on the backside. Nikolas Cosara saw the incident and rescued her.

Esta smiled up at him as they danced. "Thank you, Admiral." He was something to look at, with his remarkably broad shoulders, an imposing figure in black tunic and mask with a silver-edged cape. His eyes were turquoise and his lips very full for a man.

He smiled back. "The man has no idea how to treat a lady," he said, guiding her expertly around the floor. He was a good dancer for a sailor. Someone had taught him very well. *His mother?* It was said that he'd had a normal childhood and been made a lord by his cousin, Queen Adriana. "You dance as light as a feather, Lady."

"Why, thank you," she said, her face heating beneath the mask.

"You're obviously a local as you know who I am. That gown is stunning, by the way. It has caught my wife's eye. She has asked me to find out where you got it."

"My aunt made it." She didn't wish for Nikolas to know her identity and hoped he'd let the matter drop.

"Well, Merielle is going to want to know your aunt. Who is she?"

Dammit! He had to ask.

"If I tell you, I break my cover for tonight. You wouldn't make a lady do that would you?"

He smiled. "I don't think it fair that you know my identity and hide yours. My wife will kill me when I return empty-handed."

"I'm sure you can handle your wife, Admiral." The music stopped and Esta stepped back. "Thank you for the dance." She walked away before he could reply.

As she crossed to the buffet tables, her eyes met those of a man in a beautiful dark grey tunic with gold braid on collar and cuffs. A shiver ran down her spine and she averted her gaze. Who was he, the tall, brooding stranger in the black and gold mask?

She stood and surveyed the food, but her mind wasn't on the task. She had danced with many fine-looking men this night, but none had the magnetism of this one. She poured herself a goblet of mulled wine and sipped the warming drink until her nerves settled. His eyes were still upon her; she could feel them. She chanced another glance to where she'd last seen him, but he was gone.

* * *

Sam prowled the edges of the room, restless in his body and soul. In this room, there was someone who knew the identity of his mother. There had to be. He had spent three weeks searching out information on the girl, Vitavia, and discovered she had moved north toward Wildecoast. He had spoken to every common man and woman he could and had learned very little.

Some he had talked to said Vitavia had married and moved on. Others said they had known her, and she had had more children. None could remember her last name or the name of her supposed husband or his occupation. Now it was time to seek the nobility and discover if his mother had worked for one of them.

He had attracted the interest of one or two ladies during the evening as he had chatted around the room, but none had caught his attention; until the lady in the green dress. Her essence called to him on a primal level. His eyes were drawn to her, followed her around the room, and he had enjoyed stalking her. But now she had noticed him was it time to strike or flee? He could do with a midnight fling and masks banished inhibitions as nothing else could. Hell, if anyone knew his true identity he'd be clapped in irons and in a cell faster than he could spit.

From his enquiries during the evening, the admiral of the king's fleet was here. He had been pointed out; a tall man with enormous shoulders and blond tangled locks. His wife was a beautiful redhead who also drew Sam's eye, but for different reasons. She seemed exotic, as though she didn't belong, but he couldn't put his finger on why. They were a striking couple, but he had no desire to get any closer than a room away.

The same couldn't be said for the lady in green. He was drawn to her like metal to a lodestone and was not inclined to ignore his instincts on this occasion. If his luck ran as it normally did, she could be the link to finding his mother.

He prowled the ball room as the woman in question turned this way and that, trying to locate him. He kept groups of people between him and her until he stood directly behind her. His heart pounded as he reveled in the thrill of the chase, a feeling usually reserved for hunting ships at sea. He stepped closer until he stood behind her left shoulder.

"For whom do you search?" He growled into her ear.

* * *

Esta spun at the voice and found herself gazing up into the masked face of the man with the gold-braided tunic. He was taller than she had predicted; his eyes more piercing. A familiar niggle stirred at the base of her skull.

She took a step backward. "I search for no one, sir."

"May I have this dance?"

She swallowed hard at the thought of his arms around her. Was this her evening of excitement, her deserved treat, who stood before her? He certainly seemed to fit the bill. She nodded because she had no voice.

He grasped her hand and led her onto the dance floor. A waltz played and the man drew Esta into his arms, guiding her skillfully past the other dancers. She looked up at him once, but his eyes were so intense that she shifted focus to his chest, allowing the gold braiding to mesmerize her. What would happen when the dance was over? Would he slip from her life as quickly as he had arrived?

She glanced up at him again and found his eyes still upon her.

"You're beautiful, My Lady," he said. "No one can hold a candle to you. I find myself wishing I could see the woman behind the mask."

His voice held a deep husky tone that sent shivers up her spine. Her nerve endings were primed to respond to this man, and she wondered what it would be like to kiss those sensual lips, to feel those roughened palms on her skin.

Calluses! He had calluses on his palms. That spoke of a man of physical labor. Or perhaps a swordsman? She realized she hadn't answered.

"Ah, I don't think that would be a very wise idea." She focused on his cravat. "Your voice is familiar, have we met?"

His hands tightened on her body. "I doubt it very much. I don't spend much time at court."

"I could swear we've spoken." She allowed her eyes to wander to his face, taking in green eyes, strong jaw and sensuous lips that curved mockingly. There was something so familiar about him, not only his voice but the man himself. She frowned, willing the connection to come. Try as she might, she drew a blank.

The music finished and the man released her, took her hand in his once more and led her back to where he had found her.

He bowed. "Thank you for the dance, My Lady. I hope you have a good night."

With that he was gone, pushing through the crowd. Again, the prodding awareness surfaced. The way he walked… And then it hit her. *Samael Delacost!* It was Samael Delacost! She drew a deep breath, her heart leaping in her chest like a fish deprived of water. What was he doing here? She grabbed her skirts and ran after him, driven by a desire to speak with him; to find out why he was here. Her steps faltered when she passed through the doors to the balcony. What would she say when she caught him? He didn't know her identity and that was how she wished it to stay.

She turned to go back inside but froze when she saw him leaning on the wall outside the balcony doors. *Too late to flee!*

"Lady Moonlight, I presume?"

If her heart had pounded before, his accusation nearly burst it right from her chest.

"I don't know what you're talking about," she snapped.

"Sure, you do," he said. "It came to me as I walked away. I've been out here wondering if I should go back and find you; and here you come to me."

"I was taking some air," she said. "Naught to do with you."

"How have you been?"

"Why do you care?" she asked.

He shrugged his shoulders. "How should I know? I just do. Our adventures have brought us together. I've thought of you often over the last three weeks."

She drew a deep breath. "Well, I've not spared you a single thought."

He laughed, warm and low. "Ah, now I know that's not true, My Lady. You at least must have thought of me when you thought of your ship."

She narrowed her eyes. That he had the audacity to remind her of the loss of *Sea Sprite*, the ship she had loved and depended upon. And to think he now had two ships after his seizing of *Storm Chaser*. It wasn't fair!

"You're right," she said. "I've cursed your name every day! What are you doing in the palace?"

"That's none of your business."

"I'm making it my business. Tell me or I'll go straight to Admiral Cosara. He's here and I bet he'd be very interested to hear of your seafaring activities."

"You wouldn't dare!"

"Try me and see if I don't!"

Now it was Samael's turn to narrow his eyes. "I believe you *would* hand me in! Whatever happened to honor among thieves?"

"Thieves know no honor, Captain, and I'd love to see that smug smile wiped off your face. As far as I can see, your activities are a plague on the oceans."

"And what of your smuggling?" he hissed. "I'm sure the admiral would be interested to hear of that. Might make life a little more difficult, don't you think?"

"I have no ship so how can I be a smuggler? It would be your word against mine, and who are you but a dirty pirate?"

He frowned.

Esta could almost hear his thoughts. She knew enough about his activities to get him thrown into prison for a very long time and he didn't even know who she was. All he had was an alias to call her by and that would get him nowhere.

"Look," he said, "I don't want any trouble. I came here to get information."

"Searching out your next target?" she asked, hands on hips.

He shook his head and lifted his eyes to the stars. "I'm after information, about my mother."

She raised her brows. Did he seriously expect her to believe this? "What information?"

He took a deep breath. "I'm adopted. When I spoke of my parents the other day, it was my adoptive parents I referred to. I recently learned my real mother gave me away as a tiny babe." His shoulders slumped and a muscle tightened in his jaw.

"And you think someone here can help? Was she a member of the nobility?"

He shook his head. "No, but I've looked everywhere else and no one knows Vitavia." He speared her with the intense gaze she remembered well. "Does the name ring a bell? I thought perhaps she went to work for nobility after she gave me away. It would've been over thirty years ago."

Vitavia? It was an odd name. "It doesn't seem familiar. Have you asked here tonight?"

"I have and no one remembers her." He looked so dejected that she began to feel sorry for him. She moved closer and laid her hand on his forearm.

"This is important to you," she said.

He looked from her hand to her face. "I need to know who she is, who I am, where I came from, why I'm like I am now."

"Why does it matter?" she asked. "Is finding your mother going to make you different somehow?"

"Yes, it might," he snapped. "I've always felt an outcast, set apart from other people. The *Lenweri* and my parents are the only ones who truly accept me. Why is that? If I can find my mother and ask her why she rejected me, perhaps I can take my place in this world, instead of running away."

"That's what you think? That you're hiding from society?"

He hung his head. "More or less…"

"I never thought to hear words like that come from your mouth, Captain. I thought you loved your life, that you were happy."

He smiled derisively. "So, you see you aren't the only unhappy captain on the high seas, Moonlight."

Anger blazed within. "Don't you dare compare me to you! Don't you dare!"

He grabbed her arms and pulled her close, his breath intermingling with hers. Esta should have been frightened but, instead, she was fascinated to see what he'd do next.

"You and I aren't so different," he whispered, his breath warm against her cheek. "We both share this attraction, despite our better judgment."

"You're delusional!" She battled the desire that rose to engulf her. "I feel nothing but contempt for you."

"Let me prove you wrong, Lady." He crushed her to his chest and his lips captured hers in a heady mix of domination and sensuality.

She froze then tried to pull back, but he had her welded to his body; soon she didn't want him to stop. Even as shock coursed through her, she melted against him, her arms curling around his waist and sliding up his back. He groaned against her mouth and the vibration traveled right down to her toes. Esta sighed and his tongue slipped past her lips to ravish her mouth, the intimate exploration more than she had ever experienced. His hands slipped from her arms to her shoulders and then cradled her jaw, angling her head so he could better explore her lips and mouth.

A warm breeze swept around them as they kissed by the balcony doors and she imagined they stood on the deck of a ship, entwined in the moonlight, alone in a world of their own making. She sighed. It was so magical, she never wanted it to end. Samael crushed her closer, his hands releasing her head to slide down over the sides of her breasts. Her nipples swelled and pressed against the fabric of her gown. She leaned into him and his rod pushed at her belly. The thought of it thrusting up inside her made her heavy with need, her secret places wet.

"My Lady, we must stop here if you don't wish for me to race you into the palace garden and make sweet love to you," he said. "It's an option, I want you to know that." He smiled devilishly.

Esta's insides melted more at the desire in his eyes. He wanted her as much as she wanted him. He wouldn't when he discovered how inexperienced she was. The thought cooled her desire. What was she thinking to kiss this man in a public place and wonder what it would be like to lose herself to him?

"You're right." She stepped back and tried to straighten her dress. "I…I should go back inside, and you should…do whatever you were going to do."

He frowned as if he was disappointed. What did he expect? That she would succumb to this moment of madness? She'd only regret it later and she already had enough regrets to sink a ship.

"If you insist, Lady. I enjoyed our dance and our talk and the kiss. I'd like to spend more time with you if you'd allow it."

She stared. She couldn't spend time with him, no matter how much her traitorous body desired it. She must extricate herself before he ruined her.

"Are you mad? You shouldn't be here, and you certainly don't belong in polite society. That kiss was a moment of weakness, taken, not given freely. You must forget me as I'll certainly try to forget you. Goodnight, Captain."

She turned and fled back into the ballroom, desperate to put distance between herself and the man who had turned her night on its head. Was that what Aunt Paurella was thinking of when she mentioned a wild fling this evening? Would it be everything Paurella had suggested, or was it folly for her to think that she could ever have that excitement, that experience, in her life? Others seemed to find it. Why not her?

But she had the answer. She was a lady, an estate owner with responsibilities, even more so now that Katrine was absent and might be for months – and especially since her ship lay at the bottom of the sea, a playground for sharks and dolphins. And that man was inextricably linked with all that had gone wrong lately.

She'd do well to stay away from him, and had taken the first steps tonight. Her words had hurt him; she saw that clearly written on his face. Samael Delacost wouldn't think fondly of her after this night and she would move on with her life.

The thought almost made her weep.

* * *

Sam stood frozen after Moonlight left. Her words cut him deeper than they should have. That kiss had bound them, until he had begun to imagine the two of them together, his aching member spearing her core and sending her over the edge into ecstasy. He knew instinctively that the lady would explode like a firework; if she ever let go of her inhibitions. She kept tight hold of her feelings, but her body said otherwise.

His heart picked up pace at the memory of her pressed against him. Why had he stopped? He should have led her into the garden and pressed his advantage while he had it. She might even have succumbed. His rod was hard once more, just imagining her with skirts raised, moaning as he thrust into her and she came, screaming. Would she scream? Or would she shudder and stiffen around him, silent so as not to raise any notice?

Idiot! She rejected you, her words insulting, cold. You've no place in her world. Get your dick under control and move on!

Easy to say but difficult to do. The intriguing Lady Moonlight had wormed her way under his skin, and now he knew she was a member of court, he was even more fascinated. Of course, it meant she was further out of his reach but …

No, his head was right. She was too far above him and the sooner he realized that and moved on, the happier he'd be.

<h1 style="text-align:center">CHAPTER 10</h1>

ESTA had several dances after her encounter with Samael but her heart wasn't in it anymore. She didn't see him again and wondered if she ever would. She thought fleetingly of his search for his mother. The woman was not to be found here, she was sure. Perhaps he would never find her. It was a sad thought for he seemed to need it. Though why she should care, she didn't examine.

She decided to end her night early and was leaving the ballroom when she was stopped by Merielle Cosara. The red head was exquisite, with or without a mask.

"I had to stop you and ask about that dress," Merielle said. "It is splendid."

Esta groaned inwardly. "Thank you, Lady Cosara."

"You must call me Merielle," she said. "And you are?"

"Someone who is not often at court."

Merielle's eyes narrowed. "Ah, you wish to remain anonymous."

She nodded. "I do."

"Do you mind telling me who that man was you were with on the balcony?"

Esta's belly tightened at the unexpected question. "Why do you ask?"

"I've been watching him all night and didn't recognize him. He has the look of danger about him and I did not wish you to be at risk."

"He's looking for a woman called Vitavia. Do you know the name?"

Merielle's entire body stiffened and she speared Esta with her green eyes. "My husband's mother was Vitavia. But it could not be *that* Vitavia he looks for. She has been dead for many years."

"I'm sure there is no need to be concerned, Merielle, and don't worry, I shan't see the gentleman again."

"Ah," she said. "That is good, very good." She paused. "I will find out who you are eventually, you know."

"As you wish, Merielle. Good evening." She left before the admiral's wife could question her further.

* * *

Sam stayed out of Lady Moonlight's way for the remainder of his time at the ball. He spoke to several people. None seemed to know of Vitavia, and none interested him as much as his lady of the high seas.

His mind kept returning to what he'd wanted to occur between them on the balcony. But he wrestled it back to the reason for his presence in Wildecoast - finding his mother. At the end of an hour, he was ready to admit defeat for the night. He left the castle and returned to his lodgings in one of the better taverns close to the palace. He was discouraged but not defeated and *would* find his mother.

CHAPTER 11

THE day after the ball, Esta received a hand-delivered invitation to spend time at the Cosara estate; around a half day's travel west of Wildecoast. So, she wasn't surprised when there was a knock on her chamber door an hour later. She struggled to keep a smile on her face as she opened the door to find Merielle Cosara on her threshold.

"I have tracked you down in record time, have I not, Lady Aranati?"

She chewed her lip. "Please, call me Esta."

She couldn't help wondering where this would lead. Was there harm in making friends when she harbored such dark secrets? Did Merielle have ulterior motives for seeking her out? Esta had found in the past that ladies at court weren't renowned for their friendliness.

"I thought it was time I made some friends," Merielle said. "And I sense in you I may have one."

"That's kind of you to say, Merielle," she said, "and I'd love to visit your estate."

Merielle clapped her hands. "That is excellent. I'll summon my coach. How long until you can be ready?"

"Oh!" She was only halfway through her breakfast. Lady Cosara certainly was impulsive! "I'll have my maid pack while I finish my meal."

Merielle beamed a smile and bustled out as excited as a child on a trip to the beach. Her gut tightened. Had she made a mistake agreeing to this?

Merielle seemed desperate for friendship while Esta was content in her own company. That way, she could please herself, have leisurely breakfasts if she chose. She sighed and rang for her maid.

An hour later, the Cosara coach bounced along the western road headed for Merielle's home. On board were Esta, Merielle and their two maids. The redhead kept up a constant stream of conversation and all Esta had to do was offer a word here and there. Merielle seemed genuine and almost childlike in her naivety, but Esta sensed a latent ferocity that intrigued her.

By the time they arrived at the estate, she was desperate for a cup of tea. However, Merielle hustled out of the carriage, sent the maids to unpack and launched into a tour of the manor house. They finished in the formal dining room which was set for lunch. She immediately sat at the table.

Merielle stared, eyes wide and hand to her bosom. "I am so sorry, Esta. I didn't think. You must be famished. I'll ring for a pot of tea while we await our meal."

She sighed and relaxed against the padded backrest. "That sounds delightful."

Merielle rang a bell, spoke to her maid and then sat at the table beside her guest. "I am so excited to have you here I got carried away."

Esta smiled. "Don't concern yourself. I'm simply tired from the excitement of the ball."

Merielle leaped to her feet. She was the liveliest person Esta had ever encountered.

"I just remembered your enquiry about Vitavia." She crossed to a side table as Esta's ears pricked up. Merielle retrieved a small painting and brought it back. It was of a man and woman.

"It is so sad," Merielle said. "These are my Nikolas's parents, Vitavia and Saniste."

Esta studied the small portrait, especially the woman. She was in plain clothes but was beautiful and must have been around Esta's age in the painting. Vitavia strongly resembled Nikolas, but there was something about the woman's eyes. Something…

Could it be that Samael and this Vitavia shared that feature? She reached for the portrait and placed her fingers so only Vitavia's eyes shone back at her. She swore they were also Samael Delacost's eyes. Was she imagining it? Could she have discovered his long-lost mother?

"Tell me of the admiral's parents."

Merielle remained silent as their tea arrived. When the maid left, she spoke. "They were simple people, healers. Nikolas does not speak of them often. He feels he let them down by going to sea."

"They're both dead?"

Her hostess nodded. "They passed years ago. Saniste took a fever and died, followed by Vitavia. Nikolas was away on a mission and, when he returned, both his parents were gone."

Esta sighed. If this Vitavia was Samael's mother, he was destined for heartache. She could be, the timing seemed to fit. "How old is your husband?"

"He will be thirty-one years old very soon," Merielle said. "Why do you ask?"

"Just an idle question. Does Nikolas have any siblings?"

At this, Merielle's eyes dimmed. "He had a younger brother. Jon was lost at sea nearly two years ago."

"That is truly tragic," she murmured. "But Nikolas is lucky to have you in his life."

Merielle nodded but the sadness didn't lift. "We have each other and for that we are thankful."

Esta sipped her tea, appreciating the way the liquid warmed insides chilled by the tragic story. What should her next move be? Should she tell Samael of her suspicions regarding Vitavia? Or should she stay out of the matter and allow him to do his own investigations? If she did that, would he ever learn of this possible connection? And if not, could she live with herself knowing Samael might suffer for the rest of his life?

Why do I even care? She struggled to answer. They had a disreputable association, nothing to base a friendship on, and yet she felt more than a little responsible for his happiness. It was silly but it was a fact. Esta didn't think she could live with herself if she went back to her estate with this knowledge.

The next morning, after a restless night of little sleep and many dreams, Esta dragged on her travel gown and made her way to breakfast. Merielle was there, eating what smelled like a seafood broth. Esta hid her surprise at the strange breakfast fare and poured a cup of tea.

"You look tired," Merielle said. "Was the bed not to your liking?"

"The bed was fine," she said, as a maid brought her hot rolls, butter and honey. "I did have a terrible night, though."

"Is there anything I can do to help?"

"Perhaps." She paused, still uncertain if she should involve Merielle. She didn't know the woman well, but felt she was trustworthy - a good person to have in her corner. But if her suspicions were true, this might involve Nikolas and when pushed, Merielle would always support her husband.

"There's a man I need to find," she said, "and I can't go alone. I thought two ladies might be safer. Would you come back to Wildecoast with me?"

Merielle's eyes widened and she clapped her hands. "An adventure, excellent." She rose from the table and headed for the door. "Let me get changed and advise the staff of our plans."

Chapter 12

SAM sat at the bar in his new lodgings, having moved from a respectable tavern near the palace to one where he was more at home. The unique mix of sea water and refuse, not to mention smelly sailors, wafted to him as he drank his ale. A waitress delivered his meal and he moved to a table in the front corner, all the better to have a wall at his back and be able to observe those coming and going.

A tour of the markets this morning had revealed no clues as to the whereabouts of the mysterious Vitavia. His feet ached and he was certain the throbbing in his left little toe indicated a blister. Damned new boots! He eased the offending footwear off and peeled back his sock to find his sore toe engulfed in a bubble. He shook his head. That's what came of living on land. He didn't know how city folk bore the constant pounding on pavements that were only fit for beasts of burden.

He pushed the sore toe from his mind and wolfed down the fish pie that was a specialty of this tavern. Not as good as the last time he was here. Everything was going to the dogs in Wildecoast and he was stuck here trying to find a woman who probably didn't wish to see him. He washed down the last of the pie with his ale and ordered another mug. May as well drown his sorrows for now. That blister wasn't going back into his boot any time soon.

He had received his second mug of ale and relaxed back against the wall to enjoy it when a ruckus drew his attention to the road in front of the tavern. There was shouting and he swore he heard female voices, one that jogged his memory. Frowning, for surely the lady in question couldn't be outside this establishment, he rose and walked to the door, ale in hand, one boot off and one on.

He leaned on the door frame and looked out.

"Unhand me you lout," the lady was saying, struggling with a brutish sailor who had her by the arm. Her chestnut hair glinted in the sun and there wasn't a mask to be seen. Sam's heart gave a thump.

"What do you charge, lass?" the brute said, leering at her bosom. "I can get us a room upstairs and we can have us some fun."

"For the last time," Lady Moonlight said. "I'm not a prostitute. I'm looking for someone." She wrenched her arm again, but was no match for the man who had his heart set on a romp.

Just then, a woman with brilliant red hair interposed herself between Lady Moonlight and her brutish attacker. "You will let her go or my husband, Admiral Cosara, will hear of this."

The man laughed and motioned another sailor over. "Here's one for you, Lofty," he said, shoving Merielle Cosara at a small stocky man who stood to the side.

Lofty caught Merielle and drew her in for a kiss but the lady stamped down hard on his foot, elbowed him in the stomach and then brought her knee up under his chin with a sharp crack. Lofty slumped to his knees and toppled to the cobblestones. Three of his friends stepped up to defend him.

Sam swore. This was getting ugly fast and here he was in one shoe!

"Unhand them, swine." Sam leaped into the midst of the fracas as he pulled on his second boot. He didn't know which way to turn. Four men were more than he usually cared to tackle.

The burly sailor who had Lady Moonlight fixed Sam with an eager smile. "More than enough to go around, man. Wait your turn."

He shook his head. "Let her go," he said through gritted teeth.

"Not on your life. I've been months at sea and hankering after a tasty wench like this."

Sam took a step closer, aware that Merielle struggled with her three attackers, managing to land several punches and kicks. She was stronger than she looked. "If you want to be hung for interfering with a lady, you'll get what you wish for," he said. "Besides, this lady is mine, so I'd thank you to take your grubby paws off her."

Sam's carefully chosen words had the effect of enraging the man, but he did let go of Lady Moonlight. He threw a punch at Sam who ducked and sent one of his own crashing into the side of the sailor's head. The man fell to his knees and then collapsed onto his face. Rubbing his knuckles, Sam turned to the others only to discover Moonlight had thrown herself into the fray to rescue her friend. One man had joined Lofty on the cobblestones, clutching his groin, but the two others were dragging the women toward an alley.

Merielle screamed an odd keening as she fought tooth and nail, but Moonlight appeared to have been knocked out by her abductor. A red mist swamped Sam's vision as he took in the sight of the lady being dragged senseless into the lane. He bolted forward, smashing into Moonlight's captor and knocking him to the ground, somehow managing to save the lady from hitting her head on the cobbles. He sat her up alongside the wall of the alley and turned to the man he had knocked down. The fellow was just rising so before he could recover, Sam punched him in the jaw, sending him to the ground once more.

Lady Moonlight's chest rose and fell in a steady cadence. Sam longed to wake her, ensure she was well, but he turned to Merielle and her marauder, landing a right fist to the man's stomach and then a left to his head in quick succession. The man slumped, his hands slipping from Merielle who stood panting in the middle of the alley. She had a wild look in her eye and her hair had broken free of its confines in a mad cascade of crimson strands.

"You're safe for now, My Lady," he said, hoping to reassure her. She didn't appear to hear him but spun around to glare back at the opening of the lane. Sam glanced that way too and discovered more sailors lurked at the mouth of the alley. They looked none too happy. If they were part of the same ship's crew then he was in for the fight of his life. He flicked a glance over at Moonlight who was beginning to stir.

"You men," Sam called, trying to instill authority into his voice. "Disperse now and no one else needs to get hurt."

The crowd surged forward a step.

"Our only option is to run, sir," Merielle said.

"You run if you like but I can't leave the other lady to that mob."

"Carry her."

He turned to Merielle. "We don't have time to get to her before they get to us."

She frowned and as her eyes took in the angry men at the mouth of the alley, Sam saw fear for the first time. "Then we are done for."

"It would seem so."

There was a stir behind the crowd and a voice rang out. "What's the meaning of this? Move aside before I have all of you thrown in prison. Pick up those men and get them some help."

"Nikolas!" Merielle ran toward the mob. The crowd parted and there stood the admiral. Merielle threw herself into his arms and the sailors vanished like smoke in a high wind.

"On second thoughts," Nikolas said, turning to a man behind him. "Collect all the injured and throw them in prison. It appears they've attacked my wife." His arms around his love, the admiral met Sam's gaze. "Who are you?"

"Just someone trying to help these ladies, Admiral. They had drawn the attention of desperate men and were in a spot of bother."

"Looks like more than a spot to me." He looked down at his wife. "Have I not told you about going out in public? And who is this lady? She doesn't appear at all well."

Sam helped Lady Moonlight to her feet and supported her with an arm around her waist.

"She is my new friend, Lady Esta Aranati," Merielle said. "She was looking for someone to relay a message to, which is why we were here." Her eyes narrowed as she studied Sam. "That someone was you, wasn't it, sir?"

Sam couldn't help the reaction of his body when she said those words. Had the lady been looking for him? And to finally know her real name. Lady Aranati, indeed!

"We need to move out of this area," Nikolas snapped. "It's ready to boil over and I don't wish you to be here when it does. I thought you were safe on our estate!"

Merielle drew apart from him, her eyes flashing. "I come and go as I please, Nikolas. You know that."

The admiral drew in a long breath. "Never mind. We'll discuss this later. For the moment, we must get you and Lady Aranati back to the castle."

He turned and led Merielle back up the docks to her coach. The young driver looked fearful. "You have some explaining to do, driver. Would you let these ladies perish because you were too scared to go to their aid?"

"I'm sorry, Admiral. I was frightened. I know it was cowardly of me but since I was set upon by those men last year…"

Nikolas took another long breath. "Just take us to the castle." He turned back to Sam. "You'll come with us, since my wife believes the lady was looking for you. I'd like to question you further."

Sam was in two minds. He wished to ensure Lady Moonlight, Esta, was well, but he didn't welcome any scrutiny the admiral might provide, let alone the king. Didn't seem he had a choice. "Give me a moment to collect my things and settle my account."

* * *

Esta's mind was foggy as they traveled to the castle. She needed a pain powder and a long rest. Her body was still cold with the shock of the beating she had received and the speed at which her situation had turned deadly. She couldn't spare a thought for the man who sat beside her, staring down the admiral.

What a pickle she was in and now her true identity was at risk. She groaned at the thought band a big hand engulfed hers. She closed her eyes, not wishing to meet the prying gaze of her rescuer. How many times must she rely on this man to bail her out? *Later*. She would deal with him later when she recovered her composure.

* * *

Once at the castle, Sam scooped Moonlight up and carried her to Nikolas Cosara's private audience room on the second floor. The lady stiffened as he held her close and she remained so for the entire trip until he lay her on a lounge chair. She refused to meet his gaze as he examined her face and head. There was a nasty swelling over her right temple and puffiness around that eye too.

"Do you feel ill, My Lady," he asked. "Dizzy, weak?"

"The room is spinning, and I could empty my stomach if there was anything in it," she said, her voice warning him that she wouldn't accept his help.

"You have concussion," he said, turning to Nikolas.

"I'll have Mosard attend her right away," Nikolas said, ringing the bell.

A maid came and scurried away after a whispered conversation with the admiral. Merielle came to sit next to her on her lounge.

"I am so sorry, my friend," she said. "I was thoughtless to allow you to enter that region. We have been lucky that this man was there to help, otherwise…"

"Yes!" Nikolas said. "And this man still hasn't told me who he is."

"I'd rather not if it's all the same to you," Sam said.

Nikolas frowned. "Tell me now."

He sighed. He had known it was a mistake to enter this society; had told himself he risked everything looking for his mother in Wildecoast. But if there was a chance she might be here, he was willing to take it. Only now, his future might hinge on Nikolas Cosara.

"Samael Delacost, Admiral." He offered his hand.

Nikolas surprised him by shaking it. "Your name rings a bell," Nikolas said. "Have we met before?"

"I was at the ball two nights ago, Admiral, though I don't believe we met," Sam said, hoping to distract the admiral from delving too deep. "Perhaps someone recognized me and mentioned my name to you. I have somewhat of a reputation with the ladies in the south." Not many would associate the Singing Pirate with the name Samael Delacost, and he hoped the admiral wouldn't either.

"Perhaps," Cosara said, his gaze narrowed. "Yes, it could be that."

Doctor Mosard arrived to examine Moonlight and refreshments were delivered. Merielle set about pouring tea and serving small cakes and fruit. She then entered her sleeping chamber, no doubt to change her dirty gown.

The patient still hadn't met his eyes and Sam was becoming irritated. She was ill, yes, but he had put himself at risk, damn it, and deserved at least politeness. He hovered behind the doctor as he mixed powder in a goblet and made Moonlight drink.

"She will recover quickly with rest," Mosard said. "I'll check in again on the morrow." He bowed and left.

Sam took the opportunity to address the lady. "I seem to be making a habit of saving you," he said quietly.

Finally, she met his eyes. "Thank you."

"That's all you have to say, after what we've been through? Thank you?"

Her eyes narrowed. "I was in the docks looking for you," she snapped.

He frowned. "Why? Could it be you wanted to continue our tryst, begun the night of the ball?"

"Don't flatter yourself. I knew this was a mistake, but I thought you needed to know."

What's she talking about? The knock must have done more damage than they had suspected. "Know what?"

"Your mother, Vitavia was her name, was it not?"

"Yes…this is about my mother?"

"I have news of a woman called Vitavia who lived around these parts," she said. "I regret to inform you that she passed away some years ago."

The excitement that had gripped him at her first words now coiled around his heart, threatening to strangle the life out of it. His mother could be dead after all this?

Dread turned his voice harsh. "What do you know of her?"

Moonlight flinched. "I don't know where to begin." She pushed shaking hands through her chestnut hair, now disheveled after her misadventure. "The knowledge came by way of Lady Merielle. It might not even be your Vitavia."

At this, the admiral stalked over. "I couldn't help overhearing. Do you speak of my mother?"

Sam's gut clenched and sweat broke out over his forehead. He slowly turned to confront the admiral. "Your mother's name is Vitavia?"

He nodded. "It was. I lost her and father years back, of the fever. Why?"

It was on the tip of his tongue to tell Nikolas the truth, but he couldn't risk it here in this palace where Nikolas held all the cards. He had to get away, process this and decide on a course of action. "My mother is seeking her childhood friend after all these years. I think she might be your mother, Vitavia. She'll be sad to know Vitavia is no longer with us."

Nikolas nodded, his eyes distant as though he remembered a time when he could still count on a hug from his mother. "I give you leave to tell her. I've a likeness you may take to show her, so she may know if Vitavia is the woman she knew as a girl."

Sam swallowed his grief as Nikolas produced a battered piece of parchment which held the picture of a beautiful young woman. He couldn't take his eyes from it. This could be his mother; in fact, he was certain of it. The eyes that looked back at him were his. If this were true, Nikolas was his half-brother. It was too much to take in.

"Thank you, Admiral," he said. "This will mean much to my mother. I'll return it to you when I can."

He looked at Moonlight who frowned at him, no doubt wondering why he had lied. Perhaps it was his nature to hide the truth. Perhaps the risk of exposing himself was just too much to accept. Perhaps he was a coward after all. He knew what the lady would have done, what she no doubt wished to do now. She could expose him and let him take his chances.

All Sam wished to do was to escape the admiral's company so he could mull over this development and decide on the right course of action. He had always known the search could reveal siblings and now it seemed he had one within reach. Nikolas Cosara, leader of the King's Navy no less. How the admiral would cringe to discover he was related to sea scum such as Samael Delacost. And Nikolas would work out where he'd heard the name in time. He had to get away before that happened.

"I should be going," he told Moonlight. "I wish you a speedy recovery and thank you for the information."

The lady swallowed but didn't seem able to speak. She nodded. He drank in the sight of her laying back on the couch, wishing they had the time for a proper chat. Damned Cosara! If he wasn't so protective, they might be alone to speak candidly. He shook his head. She wouldn't wish to speak with him. She had made that very clear. He was being an idiot. He bowed and turned to leave but found the broad chest of Nikolas Cosara in his way.

"I can't let you leave without showing my appreciation, Mr. Delacost," Nikolas said. "Please name your price."

Sam smiled. "The safety of the ladies is all I require, Admiral."

"At least allow me to convey you to your home," Nikolas said.

He paused. "I live to the south and made my way here on horseback. My mount is stabled down the main street a ways. I'll have no trouble on the journey home."

"These are dangerous times to travel by oneself," Nikolas said. "And now there has been trouble, I fear retribution. I'll provide Lady Aranati my personal coach to convey her home and you may ride along with us."

He ground his teeth. "That's most kind of you, Admiral. I'm sure the trip will be more pleasant for the company."

"It's settled then," Nikolas said. "We'll leave in the morning."

CHAPTER 13

ESTA could sense the walls closing in. Her head pounded, but worse than that, she'd soon be on a trip back to her estate with Samael Delacost for company. Her feelings about that were a mix of dread and reluctant excitement, for even though she had sought him yesterday, it was only to ensure he had the chance to know more of his mother. She shouldn't care, but she did.

The man kept rescuing her and she didn't wish to be saved by any man, especially one as virile and handsome as the pirate. He was no good for her and there was no future down that road, even if he was the half-brother of the admiral. It was a mess of epic proportions.

And to add to it all was her family. Her mother was a constant concern, but now Katrine wasn't present to help her care for the aging widow. Within days of their return from the debacle of the treasure hunt, Katrine had set off to visit Hetty, the witch she had trained under. Katrine was changed since her experience with the crystal and she hoped her old mentor could shed some light on what might have occurred.

Apart from the strange glow within her sister's eyes, something else had upset her. She wouldn't talk of it, just kept saying Hetty would know what to do. Esta hoped the old witch could give Katrine solace but worried about the weeklong journey west to Brightcastle.

Yes, the next days would be an endurance test but all she could do was to limit the damage as much as possible. That meant getting rid of Samael as soon as she could. Would he tell Nikolas of their link? And if he did, what would happen? She sighed and returned to her breakfast, trying to coax her nervous stomach to accept food before she faced the music.

Esta checked her rooms one last time. There was no point in delaying any longer. It wouldn't change the fact that she must travel all day in the company of one infuriating pirate. She pulled the door closed and made her way down to the Cosara coach, which boasted gold leaf design and luxurious cushioned seats - far more lavish than her own humble conveyance.

By this evening, she'd be home, listening to her mother complain of every little thing and with the weight of the estate finances back on her shoulders. Perhaps she should stay in Wildecoast after all? It was tempting but someone had to run the estate and she was the only one putting their hand up for the task. What would she do if she stayed anyway? Worry about the chores that were going undone and the money that was not being earned and the mother whose main conversation involved criticizing Esta for the things she did wrong.

She sighed as she saw the dashing man who stood beside the carriage. Samael Delacost - the most annoying and compelling man she had ever met. Why did *he* have to be traveling with her? Curse the admiral for suggesting it.

She straightened her shoulders and marched up to him. "Good morning, Mr. Delacost. How are you?"

His eyebrows shot up and then he took her hand and kissed it. "I'm looking forward to the trip today, Lady Aranati. Might I say you look most ravishing?"

She stepped closer. "No, you may not! That's hardly the thing to say to a woman you're barely acquainted with. I'd appreciate it if you kept a civil tongue in your head."

"Ah, so that's the way it's going to be is it? Is this your way of saying you want nothing more to do with me?"

She nearly choked. "I've made it perfectly clear I want naught to do with you, Sir!"

"Mm," he said, a smirk on his lips. He did look striking in his grey suede jacket and black breeches. Broad shoulders and muscled thighs were shown to advantage. "Then why did you seek me out to tell me about Vitavia?"

Why indeed? She was still trying to work that out herself. "My conscience wouldn't allow me to keep you in the dark. That's the *only* reason." She stepped even closer. He did smell nice up this close. "Why didn't you tell the admiral that Vitavia was your mother?"

"That's none of your business, My Lady."

"Perhaps not but I'd still like to know. Don't you want a brother?"

He frowned. "Truthfully? I don't know. Perhaps it would merely add needless complications to my life, and I like things the way they are. Maybe he'd expect me to behave a certain way and I don't wish to please anyone but myself."

"You're scared," she said, suddenly seeing the child inside the man. "Why don't you tell yourself it could be wonderful, that you and he could be best friends? That it would be better than this lonely existence you lead?"

He walked a few paces away and stood staring out to sea. She followed and stood behind him, intrigued despite herself.

"Since I can remember," he said. "I've ordered my life to suit myself; even my parents couldn't control me. I don't need a brother telling me what to do, disapproving of my life." He turned to face her. "There's no way he wouldn't disapprove of me, no way at all."

She had no argument for that. Nikolas Cosara would definitely disapprove of Samael. "You could still try!"

"Well, I'm not! It would change everything and I'm not ready for that."

Someone cleared their throat nearby and she turned to find the admiral had ridden up.

"Best to be on our way, My Lady, Mr. Delacost. It is to be a long day." With that, he turned and walked his horse toward the gates of the castle.

Merielle hurried forward and embraced Esta, kissing her on both cheeks. "I have enjoyed our time together, Esta. Promise me you will come to stay when you can."

She smiled. It was overwhelming to have this woman accept her and wish to be her friend. "Thank you, Lady Cosara. I look forward to seeing you again."

Esta turned and climbed into the coach alongside her maid, cursing the formality of her words, which appeared to disappoint Merielle. The thing was, she was perfectly happy being on her own and trust didn't come easily. Perhaps in time, she and Merielle could be friends. The beautiful redhead seemed lonely. She'd try, she really would.

She turned her thoughts to the trip ahead which would have them reach her estate after dark that evening. As the coach trundled through the castle gates, escorted by ten soldiers, Nikolas and Samael, she wondered what the trip would bring.

* * *

Sam rode ahead, his eyes on the passing farmlands but his thoughts on the pickle he was in. He preferred to call it a pickle rather than admit it was more a disaster. For a man who was used to being on the ocean and free as the seagulls, he had taken steps that might see him grounded forever, especially if the admiral discovered his true identity. Already he had spied Cosara frowning at him as if trying to solve a puzzle. The man was no idiot. It wouldn't be long before he realized Sam's pirate links. Sam hoped he'd be well out to sea before the penny dropped. At least then, he might be able to elude the king's man.

Cosara rode beside him, curse him! Unlike Sam, he had his eyes firmly fixed on the dangers that might present themselves on such a journey.

"Anything specific to watch for, Admiral?" he asked.

"Dark elves," Nikolas said. "We've been too complacent in the past and the blighters are so damned sneaky. They've been more active in the north but have caused trouble close to the city in recent times. Also, those sailors who attacked the womenfolk could take it upon themselves to seek revenge. I won't be happy until we get Lady Aranati back to her estate." He looked across at Sam. "How do you know her?"

He let out a long breath. He'd known it was a mistake to start up a conversation. "We met at the ball. I told her my purpose for being there and when your lady wife mentioned Vitavia, Lady Aranati remembered my quest and sought me out."

Nikolas shook his head. "Damned nice of her, not to mention foolish. Doesn't seem the sort of thing you would do when you'd only just met a person - put herself at risk like that. Not to mention my wife."

"Your lady is pretty good at taking care of herself, isn't she?"

Nikolas frowned. "She thinks she is but Merielle doesn't understand the dangers women face when they venture into public. She's still learning."

"Oh," Sam said. This was better! Get Nikolas to answer the questions instead of him. "Why does she need to learn?"

"Merielle comes from the country where it's safer and much different. I hope she learns before something really dangerous happens. As you saw, she can be quite impulsive."

Sam nodded. "Impressive though."

"Keep your eyes to yourself," Nikolas growled, his turquoise gaze throwing sparks Sam's way.

Sam held up his hands. "Hey, your lady is safe from me. She's quite unique though." His mind wandered to the fight in the street when Merielle had almost held her own against those drunken sailors. "And she's stronger than she looks."

Nikolas grunted. "She is and let that be an end to this conversation." He turned his horse and headed for the back of the column, stopping to speak to Lady Aranati and the soldiers as he passed.

Sam watched him go. Man, the admiral got prickly when questions were asked about his wife. He smiled. That might be the key to avoiding Nikolas's questions about himself. Turn the conversation around to the bewitching Lady Merielle and Nikolas would soon give up. He nodded. Yes, that was a tactic well worth trying.

* * *

The day had been long and tiring and Esta wished for nothing more than a long soak in a hot tub. The trouble was there was no one to prepare it for her, and she certainly wouldn't ask her equally tired maid to do the honors. At least some of the preparations should be done as Samael and two of the soldiers had ridden ahead early in the evening to announce their imminent arrival.

She stepped down from the coach, aided by the admiral who also helped the maid. Now there was a man with impeccable manners! Samael, on the other hand, lounged in a chair on the side porch, a glass in one hand and the red glow of a cigar in the other. Cigars! They'd be her late father's! *How dare he!*

She turned back to the admiral. "Thank you, Lord Cosara. You've been most kind. I'll see that your room is prepared. If you'd like to send your men to the farm manager, he'll give them a meal and beds for the night. His office is beside the stables, around the back of the manor."

The admiral spoke to his sergeant who then ushered the soldiers away, taking the coach and horses with him.

"This way, Admiral," she said, glancing at Samael from the corner of her eye. As she strode to the front door, the pirate climbed to his feet and ambled over to them.

"You have a lovely home, Lady Aranati," Samael said, bowing to her.

She frowned. "Thank you, Mr. Delacost. I hope you've been comfortable in our absence?"

The door swung open and there was her mother, dressed in her best gown and with a broad smile on her face. Her mother rarely smiled.

"Esta!" she said. "I am so glad to see you." She embraced Esta more warmly than she could remember her ever doing. "And this must be the admiral? Come in, dear sir, and make yourself at home in the parlor. I have a room prepared for you and a nice supper and my best wine. I don't get to entertain very often, stuck out here as I am and with my health …"

Nicolas was swept inside and Esta was left with Samael on the porch. This was to be more of an endurance test than she had anticipated.

"Bit of a livewire, your mother," he said.

She shook her head. "Not usually. She never leaves her room and I haven't seen her dressed up since father died. I wonder what she's up to?"

"Does there have to be an ulterior motive? Perhaps she's just glad of the company."

"She has plenty of company," Esta snapped. She took a deep breath and waited for her temper to subside. "I'll go and freshen up and then meet you in the parlor, Samael." She sailed into the house and took refuge in her room.

* * *

Sam stayed on the porch for a moment, enjoying the solitude and the cigar. He had no desire to join the admiral, though he was intrigued to speak more to the woman who had produced a daughter like Moonlight. In the hours he'd been here, he had gained permission from Lady Aranati senior to explore the estate though, being dark, he hadn't been able to see much. The stables were small but neat and tidy, the horses well fed, and the fences maintained, though many would need replacing soon. Most of the outbuildings sagged under the weight of the years they'd stood. The manor house itself needed a coat of whitewash and the interior a refurbishing. There was plenty of evidence that this once fine estate needed a cash injection.

Once the cigar was finished, he wandered inside and found the parlor. Esta's mother was deep in conversation with Nikolas.

"Mr. Delacost, please pour yourself a wine. Supper will be served when Esta joins us." She resumed her conversation with the admiral, giving Sam a chance to observe the man.

He was polished in female company and listened attentively to the lady as she prattled on about court matters. It seemed her sister was the queen's seamstress and had made the striking gown that Esta had worn to the ball. The thought of Moonlight in that gown had his breeches tightening in front. He shook his head. He had to think of her as Lady Aranati or he'd give her identity away.

He returned to his study of Nikolas. He'd bet the man could carry this conversation while his mind ticked over on other subjects. He was deep and not a man to be underestimated.

"And what business are you in, Mr. Delacost?" Lady Aranati senior asked.

"Er, shipping, My Lady," Sam said, hoping that would be enough for her.

"Where are you based?"

"Costa is my home but I'm rarely there. I travel a lot, looking after my interests."

"It seems we might have much in common then, Mr. Delacost," Nikolas said.

"I know my way around a ship, Admiral."

Where are you Esta!

Nikolas Cosara smiled but his eyes were wary. Sam's gut churned at the thought of the evening ahead. The admiral had plenty of men close to hand if he chose to arrest Sam, but he wouldn't do that unless he had cause to suspect his true occupation.

Time I was back on the seas with my ship and my crew!

"Ah, Esta, there you are," Lady Aranati senior said. "I was beginning to think you had gone straight to your bed."

"And why would I do that, Mother?" she asked, giving her a kiss on the cheek. "It *has* been a long day but that's no reason to be any less the hostess." She picked up a small brass bell and rang it. "We'll all feel better for some warm food in our stomachs and a nice glass of wine."

The food arrived and Esta helped the maid lay out the platters. Sam's mouth began to water. There was fresh bread and butter, soft cheese, a thick lamb stew and a roast suckling pig with potatoes, carrots and greens.

"Help yourselves, gentlemen." Esta handed each of them a large plate and a fork.

Sam didn't have to be asked twice. He piled his plate high then seated himself at one of the small tables in the room. Half the contents were gone before he drew breath.

"This is marvelous," he said. "All your own?"

"Everything except for the spices we use to flavor the meat," Esta said.

"And the cook?"

"Has found his rightful station." Esta reached for her wine glass. "He was once a field worker but hurt himself and couldn't return to the heavy work. I suggested he try the kitchen and he has never looked back."

"A masterful idea indeed." Sam admired her lateral thinking. And if this food was anything to go by, the man had landed on his feet.

She inclined her head, accepting the praise. "It's common sense not to let good and loyal workers slip through our fingers, Mr. Delacost."

"On the contrary, Lady Aranati," Nikolas said. "I've seen many an occasion when loyal workers have been thrown on the scrapheap through injury and illness, or even old age. And then there's the case of the previous general of the king's forces who found himself on the outer after discovering his elven heritage. He's a brilliant and valuable tool and now his role has been reduced to that of advisor."

"I'm sure Kain Jazara will find his place eventually," Esta said. "He's not a man to sit back for long. You're a friend of his, are you not?"

Nikolas nodded. "I am, a close friend."

Lady Aranati senior cleared her throat. "I admit I am not acquainted with the local gossip, isolated out here as I am. How was your aunt, Esta?"

"She is well, Mother. Still creating miraculous gowns. You should have seen the dress she made me for the ball."

Sam's thoughts drifted back to that night and the moments he had shared with Esta. She had felt right in his arms and he couldn't get it out of his head. Did the fact she had sought him out mean he had a chance with her. And what did *he* want? Just a night or two? Something more lasting? He had nothing permanent to offer her, only the life of a pirate or worse, the long wait on land for her lover to return.

He sighed and Esta's eyes met his. The impact of her gaze brought a lump to his throat. His heart told him to chance it, see what might be between them. The blush that warmed her cheeks gave him hope of a small chink in her armor.

* * *

The talk of the ball continued until midnight when Lady Aranati senior took her leave. By then, Esta was almost asleep on her feet. As the maid cleared away the dishes, she showed Nikolas to his room and then returned to the parlor.

She stood in the doorway, gazing at Samael as he examined the paintings on the wall.

There was something about him that drew her, a man who would never be tamed by polite society, a man who didn't fit in, much like herself. He had saved her life on two occasions and that tied them together with bindings that would be hard to break.

"I'll show you to your room, Samael," she said.

He turned and his green gaze pinned her, stirring a deep need she had never acknowledged. "That would be most welcome, My Lady."

They walked together down the hall and she opened the last door on the right, opposite hers.

Too close to my *room!*

Samael slipped through and drew her with him. The door clicked shut and he turned the key in the lock.

Her heart raced at the thought of what he might do. Flames from the fireplace lit the room only a little. She couldn't read the intent in his gaze as he leaned over her, her back against the door and his arm resting alongside her head.

"Samael, I don't think —"

"That's your problem," he said. "You think too damned much. It's time to feel. I can see in your eyes what you want. Listen to your heart, to your body and just feel."

He lowered his head and his lips met hers, first gentle and then demanding, mastering, seeking entry. She froze with surprise but that didn't last long. His lips and tongue sent her heart racing, his wandering hands bringing her hard against him.

The sensible Esta screamed at her to stop, that this could never be anything more than a romp. Her body ignored the sober words, arching into the strength of the only man who had ever made her want more.

Her core clenched with the need to have him inside her, to welcome him to her most intimate place where no man had been. A primitive surge of desire swamped her, frightened her. What would be left of her if she succumbed to this foolish impulse? She drew back, tearing her lips from his and creating the distance she needed to think.

"You're doing it again," he growled. "Stop thinking! I can feel how much you want me; how much you need this." He crushed her to his chest, his hands molding her to the hard ridge in his breeches.

It would be so easy to take what he offered but what then?

"Yes, I want you," she said against his chest. "But what comes after when you sail off, when you leave me alone? What happens when you awaken the part of me I can never again deny?"

He stepped back and took her face in his hands, his eyes wide. "Are you a virgin, Esta?"

Her gaze fell from his. Oh, why did she have to shame herself thus? The oldest virgin in the King's Court. "Yes, but that's not what I meant."

He frowned. "Then what did you mean?"

"You've touched a part of me I've long denied, made me see the possibilities of life with a man, made me want more than I have the right to expect."

"You have every right to be happy. I wish for you to have the life you deserve, not one of drudgery where you think of everyone else before yourself."

"You can't come here and tear my world apart. It's not fair."

"Let me ask you one question." He cupped her face and forced her to look into his blazing emerald eyes. "Are you happy?"

Each word was enunciated as if it were the most important word he had ever uttered. Each of them was a blow to the foundations she'd so carefully built her life upon. Oh, why did he have to make her feel as though her life until now had been so wrong? It was a good life, a life of service, and she shouldn't be ashamed of what she had achieved.

She sighed. "No, not completely, but does that matter? When weighed against all the other things in the world like an aged mother, workers to care for and war to consider and even the animals in my care. Do I matter?"

"I deem it sad that you should even have to ask that question," he said, his gaze dulled with sadness and what looked like pity.

The only way she knew how to combat that pity was attack. Who did he think he was to call into question her decisions when he could not even be honest with his own brother? "I believe you should take stock of your own recent decisions before turning to mine!"

"Oh? And that would be?"

"Your refusal to tell the admiral you're his brother. You're both alone in this world and family should stick together."

He snorted. "Neither of us is alone. Nikolas has his wife and cousin and I have my parents and friends. Let's not be deluded into thinking either of us would be better off for having a brother in his life. I'd bring shame to him and there's a very real chance that exposing myself to Nikolas would be the end of my liberty."

"But if you could have a brother who cared for you and looked out for you, would you not wish for it?"

He smiled, the sad edge still evident. "You should know families aren't perfect entities. They bring as many problems as joys. My mother abandoned me, a helpless babe, and then chose to have two sons with another man. Why should I believe her son would welcome me?"

"Then why did you move heaven and earth to find her?"

"And that illustrates my point exactly, she's dead so there was no point."

"Samael, you have to tell him. You won't be able to stand knowing you have a brother and he being ignorant. It will eat at you and torment you until you're driven crazy by it."

She could see the picture she painted didn't sit well with the pirate. And what if one of them should perish before the relationship could be brought to light?

"Perhaps you're right," he said.

She stepped closer, sensing this was the moment to push home the advantage. "I know I am. Tell him now while you can, while you're on this estate. Nikolas will feel constrained by the rights of his hostess. Tell him before you go back to sea. It's a perilous place and you never know when your next voyage will be your last."

He drew himself up at her words. "It's not the sea that's perilous, Lady. I've faced more danger in the past three weeks than I would ever have confronted at sea. But I can appreciate the wisdom of your words. Do you truly think he could ever accept me?"

His words were wistful and in them Esta knew the truth of his feelings. Samael would dearly love to have a brother. She hoped she wasn't setting him up for failure. "I think there is every chance Nikolas will accept you but keep your occupation secret. Two surprises at once will not do. Let him build a friendship with you before you tell him you're a thief."

"It takes one to know one." He crushed her to his chest and took her lips in a kiss that soon had her forgetting what they had ever argued about. She wanted this man. Her arms slid up his chest and around his neck, binding him to her, her soft curves delighting in his hard planes. Their bodies seemed created for each other, but her practical side told her it was thus for all couples. Men and women had melded their bodies for centuries; they were formed to unite and procreate.

"Take me, Samael," she breathed. "I don't care about the future; I want you now. I want to know what it's like for a man to master me, to be a woman, nothing more, for this one night."

He lifted her into his arms and bore her to his bed, laying her down and joining her. He drew the shawl from her shoulders and raised both hands over her head, then bound her wrists and kept them there with gentle pressure from his left hand. Excitement coursed through her at the tethering, her core pulsing at what might happen now.

He kissed her, taking her lips with a mastery that left her breathless, while he ran his right hand from her neck, over her breasts and on to her abdomen. She bucked under his hand, the sensations foreign. Nipples tensed and peaked, and she was wet below, a sweet tension mounting in her belly.

His hand wandered ever lower and her restless head twisted from side to side, her knees bending and legs parting with a will of their own. She was helpless under his ministrations, biting her lip to stop the moans which rose to engulf her.

As his lips ravished her mouth, his hand slipped over her hip and down the inside of her thigh. He raised her skirt little by little, inching up to reveal her calves, then thighs then…

His hand touched her mound and she let out a screech that was quickly muffled by another kiss. He was relentless, his left hand holding her arms while his mouth and other hand ravished her. His thumb found the hard nub within her folds sending her into an upwards spiral, her core growing tighter and tighter, the pressure building until she thought she might explode. *Oh, Goddess, this is sinful!*

His lips left her mouth and suddenly they were on her slick folds, his tongue penetrating where *she* had never thought to explore, probing, thrusting – her body coiled further until something within snapped. She cried out, shuddering as wave after wave of glorious sensation swamped her. He gave her one last lick, sending shivers through her belly and she rolled onto her side, conscious she had lost dignity.

He didn't leave her but rolled her back to face him and kissed her, his mouth and tongue full of the taste of her.

She pulled back, wishing to share her wonder with him, but when she drew breath, nothing but a sob escaped. She tried again.

"That was, that was… I don't even know how to describe how I feel." Tears poured down her face and she hadn't even realized she was crying.

"Hush, my love," he said. "You don't have to speak. I can see it was a revelation for you."

She smiled. "That's exactly it - a revelation. I had no idea that relations could be so satisfying for a woman, that I would feel so…"

"Words can never adequately describe it. Like the sea, it defies words, description. Just feel, Esta. You need to feel it. Your body has been bound for so long." He untied her wrists and rubbed them, but she stopped him.

"The binding was exciting. Do you do that with all your women?"

"You really know how to throw cold water on a man," he said. "Why do you ask about other women?"

"You must have had many. You seem…experienced."

"I've had my share, but none have responded to me like you just did. You're a natural."

"Then you enjoyed it too?"

His eyes gleamed and his tongue swept across his lips. She followed it, wishing it could return to give her more pleasure. "I did."

"Can we not do it again, or other things. I wish to have you inside my body. I wish to return pleasure to you."

He groaned, burying his face in her neck. "I'm trying to be a gentleman." His words were muffled. "You're a virgin and your first time should be with someone special, not a pirate who will leave you and never come back."

"I don't care about that right now!"

He raised his head, his gaze finding hers. "You will in the morning, My Lady. In the morning you'll regret being involved with me, and if that interlude should result in a child, you'll regret it even more."

She shook her head. "You don't know me very well."

"I know you well enough and I think you should leave before we do something you'll regret." His voice was strained as though he spoke through clenched teeth.

Her heart thudded at the rejection. After all they had shared, after what he had awakened in her, she hadn't expected such cold dismissal. She flipped her skirt down over her legs and pushed herself up off the bed. Without looking at him, she left the room.

CHAPTER 14

THE breakfast room was deserted when Sam entered it the next morning. Someone had already delivered fresh tea and rolls with honey and preserves, and there was bacon in one of the silver dishes. He sighed at the domesticity of it all. For a moment last night, when he was with Esta, the possibility of a life like this had flashed before his eyes. If she would have him, that was.

This estate needed a man and one with the money to bring it back to its former glory. He had the funds, especially if he sold the ship he had kept after the incident at sea. *Storm Chaser* was still in his possession and currently being refitted and repainted. No one would ever recognize her.

He gathered some of the fare and poured himself a cup of tea. As attractive as this life might be, Sam was restless. He had found his mother or as close to her as he was like to get. There was naught to be gained from lingering. He could return to his life and she to hers. Their paths need not cross again and would not, as she now had no ship to sail on her forays. The thought of her predicament sent a wave of unease through him. How would she manage, especially with her sister away? Would the estate fall even deeper into disrepair and could it continue to support the workers? He shouldn't care. It wasn't his responsibility.

Nikolas strode into the room, his step full of restless energy.

"Good morning, Mr. Delacost," he said.

"Morning, Admiral." Great. Of all the people, it had to be Nikolas he was left alone with. And he hadn't yet decided whether to reveal his secret or not. Even if Esta thought it was a good move, he still had a niggling worry.

"What are your plans today?" Nikolas asked, as he gathered his breakfast.

"I hadn't decided though I admit I need to get back to business."

"Ah yes, shipping wasn't it?"

Sam tossed his head. "Yes, shipping."

"Pretty vague term, what sort of shipping exactly?"

"Is this any of your business?" Sam asked.

Nikolas walked over and sat at his table. "I'd say anything related to shipping does concern the admiral of the King's Navy." Nikolas's piercing turquoise stare had Sam grinding his teeth once more. If he didn't watch out, he'd have no teeth left.

"Perhaps you're right." No point in giving Nikolas more than he had to.

"Look, ever since we met that day in the alley, there's been something about you that seemed familiar."

The silence lengthened. Was this the time when he should spill his guts? He stared at Nikolas totally unable to come up with his usual dismissive jibes. "I must have one of those faces, Admiral." It sounded weak even to his ears.

"Bull! If there's a reason, tell me now," Nikolas said.

He took a deep breath and released it. "Your mother, Vitavia, was my mother too."

Nikolas shot up from the table, the chair smashing over backward and cutlery spinning to the floor. "Are you mad? Why would you say that?"

Sam remained seated but that didn't stop his heartbeat from kicking up several notches. Had he just made the biggest mistake of his life? "Calm down, man. It's true, or at least as far as I can tell."

"My mother would never have wronged my father," Nikolas spat.

"Didn't say she did. Vitavia had me before she was married. She found my parents and off-loaded me when I was only weeks old. They never saw her again."

Nikolas shook his head, hands clenched at his sides and eyes darting around the room, seeming unable to focus on anything for long. "You expect me to believe my mother had a child she never told me of? She would *never do that*!"

Sam stood. "Look, I can see this has upset you. I'm sorry."

"You are *not* my brother! And if you try to claim anything from me, I'll stomp on you so hard you'll never recover."

"Is that a threat?"

"You better believe it," Nikolas snapped.

"What's the meaning of this?" Esta stepped into the room. "Keep your voices down. Mother is still abed, and I won't have her upset."

The sight of Esta in all her glory, brown eyes blazing and chestnut hair aglow, had Sam remembering their loving last night. "Lady Aranati, I'm sorry. I was telling the admiral about Vitavia and ..."

She stiffened and glanced at Nikolas.

"So, you are party to this monumental piece of fiction?" Nikolas asked.

She drew herself up. "I don't believe it to be untrue, Admiral. Mr. Delacost looks like Vitavia; indeed, you and he share a strong resemblance too."

Nikolas shook his head. "I don't know what you people are about, but I won't have you spreading rumors about my mother. If I hear a whisper of this anywhere, I'll hunt you down and ruin you."

Sam watched a spasm seize Esta's throat. The thought of an enemy as powerful as Nikolas was enough to make even him a little nervous. Nikolas spared one last furious look in his direction and stormed from the room. Esta hurried out after him.

That's right, he thought, *go hustling after your precious admiral. Wouldn't want to let him leave without trying to mend things.*

Bitterness swept over him in a cold, powerful wave. It had been a mistake after all. His brother didn't wish to know him, in fact didn't believe him and thought he was seeking advantage. All the time he had delayed telling Nikolas, followed his gut instinct not to reveal his mother, he was right! He had listened to Esta, had let his heart guide him and been rejected. *Again.* First by his mother and then his brother.

Esta wasn't away for long. She returned, her eyes downcast. "He wouldn't listen to me."

"Smart man, I wish I was like him."

"What's that supposed to mean?"

"That I should have listened to my gut and not told Nikolas I was his brother."

"Instead of heeding my advice," she said.

"Damned right. He doesn't believe me anyway and now he's so furious, he could do untold damage to myself and my crew."

She drew her body up ramrod straight, and her eyes turned as frosty as liquid brown eyes could. "You're welcome to leave any time you wish."

"My thoughts exactly." He hesitated for a moment, not wishing to take the steps that would carry him from her presence. When she crossed her arms over her breasts and tilted her nose in the air, he knew he had better leave or face more rejection. And one of those was enough for today.

He left the breakfast room, slamming the door behind him.

* * *

Esta sat in the parlor, only the crackle of the flames in the hearth for company. At least in the past, she could escape to her ship. Now all she had was this estate that was like a stone around her throat, dragging her under. Her body had ached all day and night after the moment in Samael's rooms when he had brought her to ecstasy - then sent her away.

Why had he rejected her? What was wrong with her that he couldn't treat her like a woman, that he couldn't give her pleasure even if he was using her for his own release? She would have welcomed it as a heady sojourn from her sterile existence.

Or would she? How would she feel if he had planted his seed within her last eve? How would she deal with the possibility that she could be with child? Was it preferable never to have had that moment with him and if so, why had he awakened her at all?

And Nikolas had been furious. She couldn't have guessed the thought of an older brother would trouble him so much. Why was that? Did he really not believe Vitavia could have made a simple mistake as a young woman? That didn't condemn her.

She wished Katrine was here to talk to. Her sister was wise in the ways of men and their convoluted system of beliefs.

She couldn't believe how low she had sunk - landlocked, alone and now, perhaps, the pariah of the Wildecoast court. And what if Nikolas made it his mission to investigate the transactions on her estate? He might uncover her sordid other life and then it would all be over. She must take steps to secure her future and that of the estate. But how? She needed money. No matter how Esta tried to escape the fact, she could only see one option. She must find a suitable husband with the finances to return her estate to prosperity. And she must not delay, or the admiral might spoil everything.

She drew a sheet of parchment toward her and started making plans.

CHAPTER 15

SAM'S heart soared as a fresh breeze off the ocean welcomed him after weeks on land. Finally, he was back on the high seas with his *Lenweri* crew. They'd been glad to see him, or so he believed. It was always difficult to tell as they were a race that showed little emotion to outsiders.

The mission was simple. Sail through the night, hoping to come across an unsuspecting merchant ship or smuggler with enough expensive goods to make boarding worthwhile. The *Lenweri* could see well in the dark, making them perfectly suited for locating and boarding ships at night. Kingdom men thought them sneaky, but Sam preferred to use stealthy when describing his elven crew. He didn't know where they stood in the civil war within the *Lenweri* and didn't care. They were on his side and that was all that mattered. He was sure Nikolas Cosara wouldn't see it that way.

He swore. No matter how hard he tried he couldn't keep his half-brother out of his thoughts. It was stupid, for the man had rejected his claim outright, had taken it as an insult that he should suggest they shared a mother. Cosara was so damned uptight about Vitavia you would have thought she was the Goddess herself. Surely their mother had not been pure, or she wouldn't have found herself pregnant without a husband. It was a fact of life and Nikolas would have to face it one day. That was the only thought that gave him comfort.

There was certainly no comfort in the way he'd left things with Esta. *Lady Moonlight.* The infuriatingly beautiful, stubborn and intriguing woman he'd never be able to forget.

Never. She invaded his thoughts by day and haunted his dreams by night. The way she had responded in his room that evening had him waking from fantasies where he was sheathed in her slick heat, making her scream, sending her higher than she had ever soared. A pity it was driving him slowly insane. Had their tryst affected her in the same way, or had she put him out of her mind the second he said his goodbyes? He tried to shake off the memories but only succeeded in musing on how the lady in question was spending her time.

What would she be doing now? Tending to the myriad chores on the estate? Putting her mother to bed? Did she think of him and wonder where he was? He scoffed at that last. She would get on with her own life, drawing together what was left after the loss of her ship and Katrine's departure. But what would she do? She couldn't hope to keep the estate with the resources she currently had. That was why she had turned to smuggling. If that avenue was closed to her, what then?

She couldn't afford to buy another ship and she wouldn't cast her workers out into the cold to fend for themselves. Esta was too proud to allow the estate to descend into complete disrepair. What path would she take to save her lands and people? He swallowed the lump that lodged in his throat.

Marriage? Would she consider marriage to a wealthy man? Perhaps one who needed a young wife to bear his sons? One who wouldn't hesitate to take on an impoverished estate if he could plant his seed in a fertile womb?

With certainty, Sam knew that would be her plan. She wouldn't hesitate to cast her happiness aside and marry to save her people. Her mother wouldn't discourage it and her sister was away. By the time Lady Star returned, Esta might have taken steps she would regret for the rest of her life.

He ground his teeth at the thought of another man being Esta's first. And then he took himself in hand. He was a pirate! A wealthy pirate, granted, but a rogue nonetheless. He couldn't help her unless it was to help her into scandal.

That's why you rejected her, idiot! To save her from you! Oh, how difficult it was to recall that, when he was hundreds of leagues away.

Still, he had to remember. Down that path was ruin, for him and for Esta. He was fine just as he was. A man on his ship with the ocean for solace and his crew for company. And so many vulnerable ships to prey on. He laughed into the wind as the moon rose over his world.

* * *

Esta was in Wildecoast again. She had come up with a plan to save her estate and see it returned to its former glory. It wouldn't fail on her watch. Katrine was still absent, in fact Esta didn't know where she was or what she was doing. It was typical that Katrine would run off leaving her to solve all the problems, but if her younger sister returned her normal self, it would be worth the sacrifice.

There she was again, thinking of sacrifice. It seemed she couldn't get away from that word. And her plan would involve another sacrifice - that of giving herself to a man who had the wealth to raise her out of poverty.

The first step in her plan was a letter to the queen, requesting a "season" in Wildecoast. That would involve being away from her land for three months, a very long time to leave her business in the hands of another. And so, while she waited for a reply, she taught her estate manager everything she knew about running the business. She was hopeful, not confident, but hopeful, he would make a fair fist of taking care of things in her absence.

Her mother had been a more difficult problem. She had wished to take her to Wildecoast, in fact, Esta was sure her mother would enjoy that. Lady Aranati senior had flatly refused to leave, even for a week, let alone three months. She sighed, remembering the words she had traded with her mother. And so, a nursemaid was found to care for her, costing Esta the last of the money she had put aside over the years. Now she had nothing but what the estate could produce and sell. She shook her head wondering how she would pay the workers when wages were due at the end of the month. At least they had roofs over their heads and food in their stomachs and that was a blessing.

A reply had come from Queen Adriana in the affirmative, advising Esta that she needed a sponsor for her "season". She immediately thought of Merielle and sent her a letter requesting that favor. The reply had taken another two weeks and by then, Esta had almost lost hope that she would ever have her season. But Merielle had agreed. Nikolas was at sea on a mission and she was bored. It would be fun to have a project.

She shook her head at the thought of being someone's project. She had sent back two letters with the rider, one to the queen informing her of her arrival and one thanking Merielle and requesting a meeting at Wildecoast in one week.

And now she was in the castle with her first ball scheduled for this evening. Her Aunt Paurella bustled in with a caramel-colored gown slung over her arm. Esta could never get used to the casual way Paurella handled expensive garments.

"I'm so excited you've come for a season, Esta, and so clever to create one all of your own rather than being lost in the throng." She cast a beaming smile at her niece as she disappeared into Esta's bedchamber.

Esta sighed. She loved her aunt but at times her mother's younger sister exhausted her. "Hardly that when I'm the oldest woman ever to make her debut in Wildecoast."

Paurella reappeared. "I'm sure that's not the case and even if it was, no one will dare comment with a patron such as Merielle Cosara to look after you."

"I don't care what they say, Aunt, I really don't."

"Of course not," Paurella said. "Are you ready for the fun to begin?"

She *was* a little excited but even more nervous. She always loved a dance but this time she'd be the center of attention. She hated being the focus just about more than anything in the world. "It will be enjoyable."

Her aunt snorted. "Listen to you. You sound older than your mother. Let your hair down for once. Smile and enjoy the company of a man." She peered at Esta with eyes that were shortsighted after years of the close work needed to fashion gowns. She shook her head. "Where is the fun in your life?"

"I'm concerned for Mother," she said. "Three months is a long time for me to be away."

"I'm sure my sister will let you know if she needs you. No one is irreplaceable, dear."

"I've been told that before," she muttered, reminding herself her aunt was only being kind. "Do you know any of the men who'll attend tonight?"

Her aunt's eyes widened. "I do as a matter of fact. The queen has told me of the Master Goldsmith who lost his wife last year and is looking for a bride. She also mentioned a young lord, whose father has recently died leaving him his entire estate. Tomas Henn is his name; from the south I believe. Both will be here this evening. And there was a flurry of excitement this morning over a relative of the king's who arrived. I don't know why he's here, but it could be fortuitous."

"Now you're reaching too high, Paurella. I hardly think I'm in that league."

Paurella sighed. "Who knows the way of a man's heart, my dear? You're certainly beautiful enough to turn heads. That caramel sheath will have them swooning."

"I don't know how to thank you." Esta kissed her aunt on the cheek.

"Just be happy," she said, as she sailed out the door.

Hours later, Esta was ready. A young squire escorted her from her room to the head of the stairs that led down to the ballroom. Merielle awaited her at the foot of the stairs and she could see dancers through the double doors. The admiral's wife looked stunning in a cream satin and lace gown. She smiled up at Esta as the Master of Ceremonies announced her.

Somehow, she made it down the stairs and grasped Merielle's outstretched hands.

"It is good to see you, Esta," she said. "We are going to have such fun and you must visit my estate when there is time. I have so much planned."

Esta smiled, butterflies, or perhaps they were blackbirds, battering at her stomach, her palms sweaty. "Thank you for being my sponsor."

"It is my pleasure. With Nikolas away, I did not know what I would do until you wrote me. Since then, my mind has been a whirl of planning. I cannot wait. We will find you a suitable husband, I promise."

Esta shook her head. "It's almost too much to take in. All these people here because of me."

And thank the goddess Nikolas is away!

"Do not think too much," Merielle said. "You look beautiful and all you need to do this night is enjoy yourself."

Merielle led her through the doors and proceeded to introduce her to all the men folk there. She soon had a full dance card and spent the next hour in a mad flurry of dancing. The eyes of her partners were warm with admiration, the food was delicious and the wine she was plied with made her lightheaded.

She had danced with most of the men, including Lord Tomas Hen and the Master Goldsmith, when a man her own age approached her at a dance break. He bowed, took her hand and kissed it.

"I am Prince Piotr Zialni, Lady Aranati, and I'd be delighted if you'd dance with me."

Esta's face heated. None other than the nephew of the king! "I'd be delighted, Your Highness."

"You must call me Piotr, and I shall call you Esta," he said as he swept her toward the dance floor.

He danced well, especially for a man who carried a little weight. Piotr dressed elegantly but favored lacy sleeves. She thought they looked strange on a man. His hair was a very light brown and he would've been handsome but for the weight that made his cheeks pudgy. She was taken with a sudden urge to tweak them.

"You're very beautiful, Esta," he said as they danced a waltz. He held her close and his cologne was pleasant, but he didn't have Samael's hard strength. "I've heard your estates are in need of a cash injection."

She drew away from him a little so she could look into his pale blue eyes. "I'd rather not discuss my estates."

He crooked his head to the side. "I thought I might be able to help."

"Why would you help me, Your Highness?"

"I thought we had agreed to use first names?"

"Piotr, why would you help me?"

"As my wife, you'd have the money required to return your estate to its glory."

Esta stared. Surely, he couldn't be offering marriage. "We hardly know each other." A warning niggle wormed its way down her spine.

"I knew you were special as soon as I laid eyes on you," he said. "It's time for me to settle down and I've chosen this region to do that."

"Shouldn't we spend some time getting to know each other, Piotr?"

His eyes narrowed. "If that's what you wish, of course we can do that. Come riding with me tomorrow. We can take a hamper and have a picnic on the beach."

What choice do I have? She inclined her head. "I'll look forward to it."

"For tonight, I hope you'll save more dances for me, Lady. You move superbly." He led her to the buffet table, bowed and moved away.

She frowned after him, not sure if the proposal had been real. In her wildest dreams, she had never imagined a marriage offer on the first evening. What did such an influential man hope to gain from the union?

Merielle swept up. "Isn't this a magical night? You are the talk of the ball. Was that Piotr Zialni you were dancing with?"

She swallowed her nerves and tried to put on a bright smile. "It was. He proposed to me."

Merielle gasped, her hand flying to her mouth and her eyes wide. "He proposed?"

Esta grabbed her hand and led her out onto the terrace. "Can you keep that to yourself? I don't wish for anyone else to know."

"I do not think I can," Merielle said. "The king and queen will wish to hear of this. Piotr is under suspicion for the death of Jiseve Zialni, the king's brother. Anything he does will be treated with mistrust. You must proceed with great caution, Esta."

"I'd already gathered that. Piotr sets my teeth on edge. I wonder what he hopes to gain by his offer."

Merielle frowned. "Perhaps he wishes to be closer to the seat of power. What will you do?"

She sighed. "I can't risk making him angry. He's an heir to the throne. I'll have to play along with him until it becomes clear what else he wants."

"I do not like this, Esta. You need help. I will think on who might provide that help. In the meantime, you should spend time with your other suitors as well."

"That's good advice and I intend to do so." Esta spent the remainder of the evening dancing, trying to forget the intrigue that now had her in its grip.

* * *

A week later, she was no closer to discovering the way forward. She had spent time with Tomas Henn, the Master Goldsmith, whose name was Reid Vetta, and Piotr Zialni but she couldn't relax in the company of the latter. Even though he was as charming as the other men, the time spent with him made her shoulders ache with tension. He was perfectly behaved, softly spoken - kissing her hand was the closest he had come to expressing desire.

The same couldn't be said for Tomas Henn who had held her hand and kissed her on the cheek more than once. It was obvious he wished to do more. Tomas was funny and smart, and it appeared he had inherited a sizeable estate upon his father's recent death. He had more than enough wealth to secure a prosperous future for the Aranati family.

Reid Vetta was an older man, polished, charming and completely genuine. He was as dark as Tomas was fair, with black hair and beard, piercing blue eyes and a swarthy complexion. It was said he was a distant relative of the king. Esta enjoyed his company, especially the tour of his three shops where she delighted in the gold jewelry and other wares. Reid's wife had died in childbirth the year before, along with their baby, so he was alone. All he had were his apprentices and employees. He was a wealthy man and she was tempted by his intelligence and gentle ways.

She could see herself as wife to Tomas or Reid but not Piotr. There were others who had asked her to accompany them on outings, but she had yet to reply. Perhaps next week she would answer their notes but already her enthusiasm for this project had diminished. She longed for the peace and routine of home and hated the gossip and intrigue of court, especially when it revolved around her.

She had been summoned by the queen to luncheon yesterday and had gone, shaking in her slippers. Merielle had literally held her hand during the meeting but Adriana had seemed genuinely concerned for her welfare. The queen wanted to ensure she was safe in light of suspicions that Piotr was involved in the death of Jiseve Zialni. The queen also had no idea what Piotr hoped to gain by his marriage proposal except giving him a good reason to be close to Wildecoast. The union would allow him ready access to the king via social functions. Adriana asked her to keep seeing Piotr in case he should let something slip about his motives.

Esta was tired of it all - fed up with courting, on edge when she met Piotr and longing to make her decision so she could move on with her life. Tomas or Reid would suit her equally well but neither of them had proposed yet. If she accepted another man's proposal, she'd no longer have to see Piotr. That was why this afternoon's outing with Reid had her hopes up.

She was to meet Reid in the castle rose garden and had chosen an apricot gown that was much frillier than she preferred. She was not a frills and lace person but Paurella had suggested it. As Esta pulled on the creation, she had to admit it matched her complexion. It put her in mind of lazy spring days and the scent of roses on the warm breeze. She hoped Reid would like it.

As she was putting the finishing touches to her face and hair, there was a knock at the door. Her maid went to answer it and returned to announce that a page had arrived to escort her to the rose garden. Esta's heart picked up pace and her hands trembled as she dabbed more perfume at her wrists and throat - rose of course.

"Thank you, you may have the afternoon off," she said to her maid, then collected her matching parasol and joined the page for the walk downstairs.

This was her third visit with Reid. She found him in the garden, humming to himself as he lounged on a stone bench in the shade. He jumped up as soon as he saw her, his eyes warm as he took in her appearance.

"Esta, you look marvelous. That color is perfect on you." He kissed both her cheeks lingeringly. A warm glow of pleasure heated her stomach.

"You too look wonderful," she said, suddenly shy. What was she doing in this situation? But the answer was clear. She had no alternative and all she could do was make the best of it.

He seated her then sat, staring into her eyes. "You don't know how I've looked forward to this afternoon, my dear. You make me feel like a young man."

"You're hardly old. I would say you're in your prime." He had only a few grey hairs and, although he was a craftsman, was very fit.

"Nevertheless, you've given me my youth back."

She sensed there was more he'd like to say. At that moment, the tea arrived, and they sat in awkward silence as two maids set up a table, poured cups of tea and lifted cake and other treats onto plates. Once they were gone, Esta took a sip from her cup. At least it kept her hands busy.

He cleared his throat, but she kept her eyes lowered.

"We haven't known each other long, Esta, but I recognize what a treasure you are and…I'm so very lonely. I wondered…I wondered if you would consent to become my wife."

The cup and saucer in her hand wobbled as she placed it back on the table and turned to him. She could barely breathe, the air in her lungs seemed to have solidified. When she tried to speak, not a thing came out, so she cleared her throat and tried again.

"You're a dear man," she said, and watched fear sweep across his face. Esta didn't know herself what she would answer but it seemed Reid thought he'd be rejected. What should she say? She thought they might be content together - might even be happier than that. She had no idea where they'd live, him being a city-loving man, but surely he could practice his trade from her estate. She shook her head at her thoughts and Reid's face turned bleak. What must he be thinking?

"I'm sorry, Reid." She hurried on as he turned away. "I thank you for your proposal and, indeed, would enjoy being your wife." The words sounded strange, even to her, but he gripped her hands in his and brought them to his lips.

"Dear girl," he said. "Can it be you're consenting to marriage? I hoped beyond hope over these past days. I knew at the ball what I wanted, and I so feared another suitor would sweep in and steal you from me."

She smiled. He sounded a world more insecure than his years. Love had been unkind to this man and it was past time he had joy in his life. "Yes, Reid, I'll be your wife."

He crushed her to him, his body trembling, and when he pulled away his eyes were bright with unshed tears. "I'll make you happier than you could ever imagine, Esta. Dare I hope that you'll agree to give me a child?"

"Of course," she said. "Nothing would make me happier." In her mind's eye she saw the babe, smiling up at her with green eyes, and her stomach cramped. *No!* She swallowed down fear. *Wrong color.* His eyes would be blue like Reid's or brown like hers, not vivid ocean green like Samael's.

She pushed the pirate from her mind and concentrated on her betrothed. He would make her happy and keep her safe. He'd help restore the estate to its former glory and his occupation intrigued her. "Where will we live?"

"I have it all planned. I'll move to your home. You need to be there, and I see no reason why I couldn't live there. I can make the trip into town and stay over when I need to. There must be somewhere I can set up a workroom?"

Esta smiled. "I can think of any number of places that would be suitable." Everything was falling into place. Reid was so accommodating, and he need never know of her shady dealings in the past. The smuggling would be a secret lost forever. As long as Nikolas Cosara didn't dig anything up.

"I wish us to be married as soon as possible, dear. Would a month give you time to prepare?"

Esta drew a deep breath. A month would barely allow her to get used to the idea let alone complete all the tasks necessary, but she would have help. It was time to move on with her life, to be happy. She smiled. "One month will be suitable, Reid. I promise it will be a day for us both to remember."

Reid drew her to him and kissed her on the mouth, a gentle kiss that didn't move her at all. But perhaps he wished to keep things under control in this very public place. Any number of eyes could be upon them.

He drew back, his hands sliding from her upper arms to grasp her fingers. "I cannot believe I have such a beautiful fiancée," he said. "You'll never regret this, Esta. Never! Now I must go and make plans for our wedding and for my move. I'll see you tomorrow." He rose and hurried inside, leaving her seated on the stone bench, not sure what she was feeling.

It was sudden but marriage was what she was here for. She had thought it would take months to find a husband, had believed no one would want her. And now she was on the verge of joining her life with another.

She couldn't even imagine what that would be like. As she sat there, staring across the garden, Merielle arrived.

"There you are!" her friend said. "I couldn't find you and then someone told me you had met Reid here." She looked exquisite in a russet satin gown with lace overskirt. Her shoulders were bare, and she wore lace gloves in the same color. "Esta?"

"Oh," she said, shaking herself out of her reverie. "Hello."

"You seem not yourself," Merielle said. "Where is Reid?"

"Gone," she said. "He had things to attend to."

"Such as?"

"A wedding feast…ours."

Merielle squealed, the sound slicing through Esta's ears. As she tried to recover from the noise, Merielle drew her to her feet and danced her round and round the small patch of grass in front of the bench.

"Congratulations!" She drew Esta back to the seat. "Tell me all about it."

"There's not much to tell. I met Reid here and he asked me to become his wife. We'll live on my estate and it will be perfect. Just as I'd always hoped."

Merielle's eyes danced. "You'll adore being married. Nikolas excites me so much I dread being apart from him. Since we met, he has been all I've thought of. Love is a treasure beyond price."

Esta thought of her recent moments with Reid. She was excited to be getting married but Reid himself hadn't excited her. Maybe more time spent together would solve that problem? Or perhaps Reid was waiting for true solitude before he made her heart dance and her body sing? Either way, this union was something to celebrate.

"I can't wait, and I have you to thank for helping me," she said. "I wondered if I could ask another favor?" She didn't like asking for help but in this case, she needed Merielle if she was going to be married inside a month.

"Of course, I will be happy to be your matron of honor, Esta." Merielle wrapped her in another hug.

"Oh, yes." She would need a matron of honor and with Katrine away, Merielle was the only other woman suitable. "Thank you."

"And I will help you with the ceremony and the marriage feast. We must decide where it is all to take place. Also, I will speak to Reid about the food and drink and you and I must decide on our dresses. Oh, there is so much to plan. When is it?"

"In a month."

Merielle's hand flew to her mouth. "Quick, we must go and see your aunt about gowns." She pulled Esta off the bench and hustled her into the castle.

Chapter 16

SAM dodged a sword to the head and rammed the butt of his weapon into his opponent's temple. As the bearded man slumped to the deck, Sam stood over him gasping. *Man, I need to work on my fitness!* What was the deal with all this resistance? He surveyed the deck, relieved to see the *Lenweri* had subdued most of the crew. They'd tied them up and herded them into a huddle in the middle of the deck.

He grabbed a length of line and bound the man he'd fought with, then dragged him over to the others. "Where's your captain?"

"That's 'im you just clobbered, scum," one of the crew said, spitting at Sam's feet.

"I don't want any more trouble," Sam said. "We'll take what we came for and leave you to get on with your day." The sun was cresting the horizon and it was past time for them to be gone.

"You'll regret this, pirate," the same man said. "The captain has connections up high in Wildecoast. He'll have the admiral after you for this."

Sam held his tongue and walked away. Usually the ships he targeted had crews that capitulated easily, but this captain had obviously given the order to fight. He didn't like hurting people. His strategy of nighttime boardings and strange *Lenweri* crew were usually enough to minimize any resistance. But not this time. Several of this ship's crew were dead or badly injured and that might bring him to Nikolas Cosara's notice.

The hold revealed rich bolts of cloth, expensive wines and a small chest full of gold coins, amongst other larger items such as tapestries.

He set about organizing the removal of anything they could easily carry from the hold into several waiting boats. The ordeal had left him deflated when he usually seethed with excitement. There was naught better than surveying the hold of a boarded ship, wondering what treasures might lie there.

He returned to the *Silver Lady* with the first of the treasure, only half concentrating on the task at hand. His mind was on the reason for his melancholy. Was it the threat of attention from the admiral, or the reminder that his half-brother had rejected him? Or perhaps he was becoming jaded with this life. The thought of settling down somewhere, anywhere, had been with him lately; his dreams filled with a wife and children when he had never contemplated that before. Often the woman in his dreams looked very much like Esta.

But he had destroyed the friendship they shared, if you could even call it that. He cared for her far more than was healthy. So many times, he'd found himself regretting he'd not taken her that night at her estate. His body yearned for her and he imagined how magical it could have been. But despite what they'd shared and the connection he had with her, he knew, in his heart, she was destined for a life that had little to do with his.

Except he was worried. What would she do now her boat sat at the bottom of the ocean? A shiver ran through him as he imagined the loss of his own *Silver Lady*. It didn't bear thinking of. Perhaps he should've given her *Storm Chaser* instead of adding it to his list of assets. He'd been selfish. The least he could've done was offered Esta the other ship.

He paced up and down his deck as the *Lenweri* brought the rest of the haul aboard and raised the rowboats. He was filled with a restless energy that had naught to do with the recent fight. Nande approached, the early morning light revealing his cat-like irises.

"All are aboard, Captain," he said. Instead of asking for orders, he studied Sam. "You are uneasy."

Sam shook his head. "It's nothing, Nande." He stared at the elf, thinking it would be nice to have a friend he could share things with. "Can I ask you something?"

Nande frowned. "Of course."

"Do you think I should have given *Storm Chaser* to Lady Moonlight?"

"Why would you do that, Captain?" Nande looked as puzzled as an elf ever looked.

"She lost her ship and I know how that feels. I worry for her." His voice dropped at the last.

"Worry?" Nande appeared positively alarmed. "You never worry."

He sighed. "I do now. Answer my question if you will."

"On this I cannot advise. You owe the lady nothing as far as elven law dictates, but human niceties are tricky, especially where women are concerned. I mean no disrespect."

"Then tell me what you perceive about the ship we just plundered. Will it bring trouble?"

"Men died."

Sam ground his teeth. "Will it bring trouble?"

Nande shrugged. "I would advise lying low for a time or we could move our activities further up or down the coast."

"I wonder if I have the stomach for this life anymore."

Nande placed his hand on Sam's shoulder. "This time will pass, and you will again feel the freedom of the ocean and the lure of treasure. If you would confide in me, perhaps I could advise you better. Come, we sail for home. The crew needs a rest."

As Nande walked away, Sam stared after him. For an elf, that was a long speech. Somehow his second-in-command had discerned his recent troubles, even if he didn't know the specifics. How would his life look if he gave up the ocean? Could he walk away from the freedom he'd always loved? If Nikolas caught him, he'd be forced to, perhaps even be thrown in prison for the rest of his days.

He took a breath and forced his thoughts to the present. They had goods to sell. He'd sail down the coast to Shawmere, the southernmost port in Thorius. By the time he had offloaded his cargo, it might be safe to return to the sea.

* * *

Esta rose from her bed on the Cosara estate and stretched her arms above her head. The two weeks since her betrothal had flown by in a haze of decisions, dress fittings and snatched moments with Reid. Now she was having a much-needed break before returning to Wildecoast to complete the preparations. She smiled at the sheep in the rich late summer pastures, realizing how much she had missed the rural life. Lucky for her, her husband-to-be intended to move to her estate after the wedding.

They had decided to marry on the Aranati estate, making the whole process easier for her mother to attend. Paurella was making a new gown for Lady Aranati senior, who, when Esta had visited her last week, said she was overjoyed that her daughter was finally to marry. Reid had made funds available to prepare the estate for the event. A team of painters, carpenters and gardeners would labor night and day for the next two weeks, so her home was presentable.

Reid had accommodated her every wish, asked her opinion in all decisions and given her a magnificent ruby and diamond engagement ring. It sparkled in the early morning sun, reminding her of her new life which was about to start. She was so fortunate to have family, property and a man to love and take care of her. Her life had been completely turned around and now she might finally live like a normal person.

Why then did she have a nagging dread within? Over the last two weeks, she had ruthlessly pushed all doubts aside, determined to have everything life had promised but never delivered. She had no reason to fear the future. Except that she didn't love Reid. Perhaps she could grow to love him and already she cared very deeply for the gentle goldsmith, but he didn't move her. And whenever she had that thought, her mind flew to Samael and his unruly ways, his sudden smiles, his passion and zest for life.

Esta had had passion once, before life weighed her down. Her time with Samael had made her see there was more to life than duty; that true passion might still be possible. If only she could be truly free to love and be loved by her one true soul mate. What if it were possible? Was she deluding herself that a love match would lead to greater happiness than would a marriage of convenience? Her mother had loved her father desperately and his loss had left her a shell of a woman. It was sad. Perhaps Reid was a safer option than a passionate, fiery romance that would leave her desolate when it ended?

And where was Katrine? Esta had sent letters everywhere she could think of and had heard nothing. At this rate, she'd miss the happy event, though she would be furious Merielle had appointed herself matron of honor.

Ahh! Her life was still much too complicated.

She opened her wardrobe and surveyed the gowns Merielle had hung there. A few were her own but many more belonged to the admiral's wife. They were, happily, similar in size and height and even their coloring wasn't much different.

She pulled out a pale green gown with white lace sleeves and a gold band at the waist. She did love beautiful gowns and this one was simple but elegant. The effect when she surveyed herself in the mirror took her breath away. Esta could almost believe she was beautiful.

She brushed her hair until it shone and fixed it in an elegant twist. Gold slippers completed the outfit and she left her chambers for the breakfast room. Today she and Merielle would finalize the guest list and send out the invitations, though most guests knew of the event already. Her hostess was already in attendance when Esta entered the room.

"Good morning," she said. "Oh! That gown is divine on you. I insist you keep it. I have so many and Nikolas is always commissioning new ones. I can't possibly wear them all."

"Really? I must admit I do love it."

"Then keep it," Merielle said. "Now that is settled, we will get to this list." She bent her head over a sheet of parchment and Esta smiled. This woman had come to be a good friend over the last three weeks. Esta loved her dearly despite their differences, or perhaps because of them. Merielle had a sense of fun and joy in life that Esta envied. She was happier, more carefree when in her company.

Esta poured herself a cup of tea and sat down to hot rolls with honey. Over more cups of tea, they soon had the list completed.

"It seems so many," Esta said, her stomach tight with the thought of all the guests she'd have to welcome and cater for.

"Do not worry, my friend. Reid has everything arranged. All you will have to do is be beautiful and alluring as all brides are."

"What was your wedding like, Merielle?"

She grimaced. "Huge. I was new to town and everything was bigger and louder and more confronting than I had ever imagined. Nikolas was wonderful. He kept me calm. The ceremony was at the castle, of course, and everyone was there. I wore a cream sheath of satin and lace with a train five paces long. I tripped on it so many times, I am sure I was the biggest entertainment."

"It must have been daunting," Esta said. "Where did you come from?"

Merielle frowned. "I don't like to think of where I came from." Her voice had gone quiet and some of the joy seemed to leach out of her. "It was very different from the world I now inhabit."

Esta sensed there was a story behind those words and longed to hear what trials could so affect her beautiful friend. "Perhaps one day you'll feel ready to tell me of it."

"Perhaps."

Merielle didn't sound at all sure that day would come. She fell silent but then appeared to shake off her melancholy. "I shall ring for more tea and we can finalize the menu. You will be far better at that than I. My tastes are a little strange at times."

Esta had noticed Merielle's odd palate, preferring sea food on the raw side and shunning meat and vegetables. It didn't make sense but Esta had become used to her quaint habits. "I've a good idea of what the menu should look like. A buffet will be best, and we'll choose a wide range of meats and fish as well as hot dishes and breads."

They still had their heads together, laughing over one of Merielle's dessert suggestions, when the sound of boots came from the hall. Esta glanced up to meet the hostile eyes of Nikolas Cosara.

Merielle pushed herself up from the chair and flung herself into his arms. He clasped her tightly and a pang of jealousy gripped Esta. She wanted that love for herself…oh, not Nikolas, but the devoted and passionate love of a strong man who would meet her halfway.

Merielle wiped her eyes as she stood back to admire her husband. "You have lost weight, darling," she said. "It is fortunate you are back early. Imagine what another week at sea would have done to your body."

His body looked fine to Esta, more than fine. Why, if she looked at Nikolas with eyes half-closed, she could almost imagine… she pulled herself up short. She should not be looking at Merielle's husband like that, even if she were imagining another, similar man. *Goddess, I should look at no other man but Reid!*

Reid, Reid! Her face heated under the admiral's scrutiny.

"Lady Aranati," Nikolas said. "I didn't expect you here. To what do we owe the pleasure?"

"Let me tell him." Merielle pulled Nikolas to the table and poured him a cup of tea. She ushered him into a seat and heaped a plate with pastries. "Esta is to be married to a fine man. You may know him - Reid Vetta, the Master Goldsmith."

"I do know him." Nikolas relaxed into his chair. "When is the happy event?"

"In two weeks, Admiral," Esta said. "I'm pleased you returned early, so you could be a part of it. Merielle wouldn't wish to be there alone."

"No, I did not but now it is no longer a concern." She frowned. "Unless you are to leave again very soon. Are you?"

"That depends on several things." Nikolas stared at Esta as if she was the key.

"You must tell us over lunch," Merielle said. "If you will excuse me, I shall go and make sure the meal is ready." She bustled out, not seeming to notice the tension between her husband and friend.

"I have a question for you, Lady Aranati." Nikolas fixed her with an icy stare. "Where is Samael Delacost?"

She sat up straight but couldn't stop her fingers fiddling with the parchment before her. "I have no knowledge of his whereabouts." What did he think she was? The man's keeper?

"Ah, but you could take an educated guess, could you not?"

Esta didn't know what to think but she was not about to reveal Samael to his brother. She had already done enough harm. "I have no idea. Where do *you* think he is?"

Nikolas laughed. "Perhaps you don't know at that. I had a nagging feeling that I'd heard of Samael Delacost before, but I couldn't remember where. It's tickled my mind ever since we met. Then over the last two weeks, there's been an increase in piracy on the seas I control. Violent acts by these pirates have killed and maimed honest merchants plying their trade between Shawmere and Eagle's Reach. The name on everyone's lips is the Singing Pirate. I've heard that name linked with Samael Delacost."

She feigned shock. "I had no idea. Are you sure?"

His hand hit the table and Esta jumped. "You know damned well who that man is. I wonder how you came to know a pirate. I also wonder what I'd find if I delved into your finances, Lady Aranati, so you'd better cooperate with me or I'll have the royal accountants go through your ledgers."

She couldn't hide her dismay, not to this man who seemed to read her like a book. "I'd rather not tell you how I know Samael."

"I thought not." He paused, watching her like a seagull watches a fish. "Listen, I don't wish to cause trouble for you, however I can't have this man raiding the seas to his heart's content, especially when people are being hurt."

"That doesn't sound like him," she said. "Are you sure?"

"As sure as I can be. He has a *Lenweri* crew."

Esta sighed. "Perhaps there's another captain using elven sailors?"

Nikolas merely raised one brow and fixed her with a stare that chilled her belly. She tried to remain silent, to wait for him to take the lead, but in the end, she couldn't endure it any longer.

"What do you want of me?"

"You're the only link I have with him at the moment. I want you to help me find him before he causes more trouble."

Her heart threatened to beat its way out of her chest. "What will you do with him?"

"Prison for the rest of his life if he's guilty."

She took a deep breath and closed her eyes, battling feelings she shouldn't have for any man besides Reid. Was this her moment of choice? A critical moment when she must choose the correct path or forever regret? Could she truly leave her old life behind, turn her back on the man who had saved her more than once? Did she owe him anything?

"I'm waiting for your decision, Lady," Nikolas said.

Esta's eyes flashed open to take in his uncompromising visage. "Do you feel naught for your brother?"

"You'll not mention that again!"

"Open your eyes, man," she snapped. "He's the image of Vitavia, and you and he share many features. If you weren't so stubborn you could've acknowledged him weeks ago and maybe this wouldn't be happening. I lay this at your feet!"

Her words silenced him and Merielle walked back into a room thick with tension.

She looked from one to the other. "What are you fighting about?"

Esta rose. "I'll leave you to talk." She kissed Merielle's cheek. "Call me when you're ready for lunch."

"You're not leaving until I know what this is about," Merielle said, surprising Esta with the edge of steel that infused her words.

Esta looked at Nikolas. "Should I tell her, or will you?"

He sighed and stood. They waited as he paced the length of the room and back. Finally, he turned to Merielle. "I have reason to believe Samael Delacost is my half-brother."

Merielle gasped, her hands flying to her mouth and tears springing to her eyes. She let out a long breath. "That is the most wonderful news I have had since Esta told me Reid had proposed. I thought he looked familiar. Now I know he reminded me of you." She went to her husband and pulled him into her arms. His eyes found Esta's as he cradled his wife.

"I don't understand," Merielle said, pulling back. "What is there to argue about?"

Nikolas frowned. "I don't wish to admit he's my brother."

"Why?" she asked. "You have no immediate family. This man is a gift from the Goddess. Remember how lonely you were before I came along?"

"He's a pirate, damn it!" Nikolas snapped. "I can't have a brother who's a thief, not in my position."

Merielle frowned. "Oh, well, I can see that might be awkward… but he *is* your brother. How could you allow something so trivial to come between you? You would never have allowed this with Jon."

Nikolas's face turned red. "You of all people should know better than to bring my little brother into this. How dare you!"

Esta wished the floor would open and swallow her. But it was intriguing. There was some issue over Jon that caused trouble for this pair of lovebirds.

"I am sorry, beloved," Merielle said. "You are right of course. But the fact remains. You need this man."

"Need him like a hole in the head!" Nikolas pulled away to pace back and forth across the room, his fists bunched at his side. "When I think of what the king and queen will say when they hear…"

Esta moved in front of him to halt his restless pacing. It was careless of her for she hardly knew the man and didn't know how he'd react to anything she did. "Don't tell them," she said. "Please?"

He scowled. "What's he to you? Why do you care?"

She swallowed her fear. "I owe him for my life. You can't bring trouble down upon him. It was at my insistence that he even told you he was your brother."

Nikolas looked skyward, shaking his head. "So, you feel guilty. It's not your fault. He's the one boarding ships and robbing people. I would've been drawn into this eventually."

"What will you do?" she asked.

He took a deep breath, looked at Merielle and then at her. "I'm going after him."

"I wish you would reconsider," Merielle said.

"I'm going with you —"The words were out of Esta's mouth before she had time to think. She clamped her jaw shut to stop more impulsive decisions escaping. But when she thought about her alternatives, she realized it was the only thing to do.

Merielle gasped. "You cannot go, Esta, you have a wedding to attend."

She looked at Nikolas. "We may be back before then."

He shook his head. "I wouldn't count on it. This will be an open-ended mission. No way to tell how long it will take."

The enormity of what she'd said was beginning to dawn on her. She was about to postpone her wedding to sail off in search of a man who should mean nothing.

Oh yes, Samael Delacost had saved her and made her heart race; had brought more excitement to her in a few short days than she had known in her entire life before meeting him. Who was she deceiving? He was important to her or she wouldn't even consider upsetting Reid and risking everything she had worked on for the last weeks and months.

As she stared into space, Merielle's firm grip on her arm brought her back to the moment.

"Please, Esta, you cannot take to the high seas in pursuit of this man."

She huffed out a breath. "I thought you'd support me, knowing how important this is for your husband."

"You cannot throw everything away now. Nikolas has enough sailors to help him find his brother. He doesn't need you." She turned to her husband. "Tell her not to be silly."

"If she wishes to come, I'll not stop her. I suspect Lady Aranati might have an idea of where I might find the pirate."

Merielle scooted back to her husband. If she were not so appalled at what she had just offered to do, Esta could have giggled at the sight of her hostess, upset and desperate, flying from one to the other, trying to convince them she was the only sane person in the room.

"Why now, Nikolas? If you must chase after your brother, why must you go now? Wait until after the wedding. Reid will not understand. I just know Esta is risking everything."

Nikolas's face hardened. "Her choice. And stop calling him my brother. I'd rather not think of him that way."

Merielle's fists bunched and her body trembled. Esta thought she might strike Nikolas. "You are so stubborn. Why am I surrounded by stubborn people?" She stared at her husband for long moments, then spun and left the room, slamming the door.

Nikolas looked at her. "If you really mean to accompany me in the search, be ready to leave in fifteen minutes." He too left the room, the heels of his boots echoing down the hall.

Esta paused for mere moments before following. She had made her decision, or her heart had, and now it remained for her to see if she could save Samael from himself and bring the brothers together.

Chapter 17

SAM was on his ship sailing through high seas to the north. He had offloaded his goods and received a handsome price in Shawmere, then spent a week repairing and cleaning *Silver Lady*. By now, a week down the track, it should be safe to return to one of his secret harbors.

They had a smooth run north despite the big swells and he was looking forward to reaching his island home, Pirate's Rest. It was his most used retreat, an island shaped like a horseshoe with deep water mooring and a narrow channel out to the open sea. He had makeshift huts there and permanent fire pits. Inland was a spectacular waterfall where he liked to swim. Over the years, he had planted all manner of fruit trees and they had thrived in the sheltered spot. He dreaded the day when it was claimed by another pirate, but so far, they'd only detected the occasional visit by others.

As they neared the island, he gave the order to trim the sail, so they could prepare for entry into the narrow channel that led to the harbor. Navigating that channel was a task many captains would shun. That was why he had this haven to himself. A ship of *Silver Lady's* size shouldn't be forced to squeeze through these towering cliffs, but he'd never scraped even one splinter off her hull. The *Lenweri* were gifted sailors and without them, the task would've been more difficult.

He smiled as he looked forward to the next few days, lying in a hammock in the sun, partaking of the sweet fruits of his labor, both on the island and those he had purchased in Shawmere. He deserved his reward - he did. He had mouths to feed. One day he'd retire and perhaps enter the world of legitimacy, but not yet. Not after his experiences in Wildecoast and with his brother. That place was more dangerous than the high seas by far, for his life and his heart.

Esta Aranati. Where was she at this moment? Was she still slaving away on her estate? Even he could tell that wouldn't last forever. Sooner or later there'd be a tough season and the farm would fail. He hated to think of Esta going hungry, scouring her books to find the savings that would allow her farm to function for another year. But she had other options. She could marry a rich man before she was too old to have children and so save her lands and people. He saw in his mind's eye a contented Esta, surrounded by her children, an older husband by her side. Any man would be proud to call her wife - except him.

The thought struck at his belly like a knife wound. He could have saved her estate, given her a ship, but he couldn't give her himself and that was what she needed more than anything in this world. She needed a partner to help her in life. He could never be that man, not if he gave up the life of a pirate, not if he turned his back on the ocean and lived the rest of his days on land. It wasn't in him. And so, he'd never see her again. He couldn't bear to see her with another man, a man who might make her happy and secure but not excite her as he knew he could.

Damn it! His thoughts were whirling round and round, telling him the same things they always did. But his heart was with Esta. Somehow, he'd have to convince his heart to give her up. And while he was at it, he'd convince his soul to stop hoping for a brother to fill that void he seemed to have - that had always been there. The missing piece of the puzzle he could never quite find. *Nikolas.*

The mouth of the harbor opened before him and Nande turned the ship into it without a word from Sam. Tonight they would feast on pig and he'd drink until the thoughts of all that he might have had were silenced.

* * *

Esta knew freedom for the first time in weeks as she breathed in the salty spray picked up by the freshening wind. She longed to take the wheel and send this beauty over the waves, but couldn't give away her sailing knowledge. Already it had been nigh on impossible to hide her familiarity. Nikolas's eyes were constantly upon her, as if he tried to solve a difficult puzzle.

She looked up at the foretop castle, where her sister perched, and they shared a smile. Katrine was waiting for her in Wildecoast when she and Nikolas returned from his estate. It was as if she had known Esta needed her, but in reality, she had returned home to the news of the wedding and set out in search of her older sister. Mother would have been pleased about that; Katrine had spent only one night with her before setting off for Wildecoast.

The two women were attired in breeches and tunic with white undershirts and scarves to keep their hair tidy. Esta wore an orange satin sash around her waist and had knives tucked into her boots. The sailors had laughed when they boarded but one look from Katrine had silenced them. Esta didn't care how her sister had changed, as long as she was here with her, but there might be trouble from those who feared her silver-flecked eyes.

Her stomach churned like a bucket of bait fish. They hunted Samael. What would he do if they found him? Would he run from them and perhaps risk his life and that of his crew?

She couldn't see him surrendering without a fight and of that she was terrified. Not for her own life but for the man who had been her savior. Hanging onto a line, she closed her eyes and recalled all the occasions when he had moved her. Samael Delacost had gotten under her skin and there was no digging him out. Was there a deep hidden part of her that still longed for a life with him?

She opened her eyes to her sister's bright silver gaze.

"Are you well?" Katrine asked.

"I should be the one to ask you that." She searched Katrine's face for signs of deeper changes. She sighed. "I'm in such a bind, Katrine."

"You love the pirate."

Esta's head snapped up. "I wouldn't call it love."

"I would, and he loves you. Anyone who is close to you can feel the connection. I would caution against it, but I think I should save my breath. You'll do what you wish and so will he. I hope you can find common ground, or two souls may be destroyed."

Esta frowned. "What has Hetty done to you?" She referred to the witch Katrine had turned to after the debacle of the crystal cave.

Katrine stepped closer, her breath hissing through her teeth and her eyes snapping sparks. "Don't mention her name in public. I don't wish anyone to know I'm associated with her. She'd be in danger."

"I still ask the question."

"I've completed my training. The crystal has enhanced my abilities. I may become the strongest of my kind my mentor has ever seen."

At her words, fear looped tight around Esta's heart. "How are you supposed to live a normal life?"

"I can't care. This is the lot I've been handed, and I must make the most of it. I've already accepted that I'll be alone."

"Then it will be the two of us alone together." She hugged her younger sibling. Katrine stiffened, then relaxed into the embrace. They stayed like that for long moments and Esta's heart was lighter when they parted.

"It might not be too late for Reid," Katrine said.

"You didn't see his face when I told him I had to delay the ceremony. He was furious and the cost is only part of the reason. I've made him lose face before his peers and the community. He's a gentle but proud man. I almost wept for him."

"But not for you?"

"Katrine, you know Reid and I were a marriage of convenience. I'm fond of him and hoped I'd grow to love him. I have to face the possibility that I've done irreparable damage to our union."

"Your actions speak louder than your words. You're charging out to sea in pursuit of a man who might not appreciate your help and leaving your betrothed to pull together the shards of his pride."

"Thank you for your support, Sister," Esta said, dismayed at Katrine's brutal summary of her actions. "I know my behavior is telling but I couldn't turn my back on Samael. I'm afraid that Nikolas will go too far without my involvement."

"Again, the control complex," Katrine said, a smirk on her face. "You don't trust the admiral will deal fairly with his own brother?"

"You didn't see them together and you didn't see the fury on Lord Cosara's face when he told me of Samael's latest activities. I must be present at their confrontation so I can try to bail Samael out if needed. I owe him."

"You owe him nothing as far as I see it. I don't think you know what you want. First you get a fixation on Samael and then you accept a marriage proposal. Now, you run off to find the rogue, leaving your betrothed's life in tatters. You're behaving like a child, not a mature woman. When are you going to decide what you want and go after it?"

Esta glared at her sister. "Perhaps that's what I'm finally doing. I don't know if this is love. I just know I must find him. If it ends up a big mess, perhaps I'll throw myself on Reid's mercy."

"Do you hear yourself? Forget Reid or turn this ship around if you can't do that. Make a decision and stick to it. You can't have it all your own way."

"As far as I can see, I've never had my own way," Esta snapped, thinking of all the years she had looked after their mother and the estate - all the worries she had shouldered while Katrine was away learning her craft. "Perhaps this is me being selfish for a change."

"You said it, not me."

"Is there anything I can do to help, ladies?" The deep voice of Nikolas Cosara caused Esta to pull herself back into line.

"Merely a sisterly chat, Admiral," Katrine said, her eyes averted.

"I don't want any trouble on this ship, even if it *is* between siblings." Nikolas locked eyes with Esta. "I wanted to ask you to my cabin to peruse the maps, if you please, Lady Aranati."

She nodded and followed him below. His cabin was neat, the maps laid out on a desk before the rear window. She reminded herself not to show too much knowledge as she scanned the maps, marking off in her mind the places they had already searched.

"I hope you're not leading me on a wild goose chase, My Lady," he said, a muscle ticking in his jaw.

Esta sent him a look that she hoped would cut him to the quick, but his turquoise eyes grew colder. "I wish to find the man as much as you do, Admiral. There's no way for me to know what harbor Delacost might use for his refuge. It's a process of elimination and we have several more to search."

"I wonder how you came upon such knowledge. You seem very conversant with this ship."

"It's not so hard to understand. My father was fond of sailing and took me on many trips. He showed me the islands in this region." She shut her mouth before she gave away too much information. It was true. Father had taken her on several voyages and imbued in her a love of the ocean and sailing. Sadness washed over her leaving her drained. She did so wish this could be over so she could move forward, with or without a man in her life.

Nikolas jammed his finger on the map. "This seems a likely target, though it would be tricky. The access to the harbor is through a narrow channel. A ship could barely get through in good conditions without scraping its hull and risking disaster."

As Esta peered at the horseshoe-shaped island, a tingle ran down her spine. Samael was a superb sailor and it'd be just like him to take on the tricky task of navigating the channel. "I never heard him speak of it, but this could be it. If so, he might be holed up there as we speak. How do we find out?"

"We won't be able to check his presence without alerting him, but that channel would need to be negotiated as the tide was going in, at least on the inward run it would. It's ideal conditions in the next few hours for us and he'd be trapped."

"What if we sail in and he's not there?"

"That's a risk we have to take," Nikolas said. "I'd rather trap him in a harbor than fight him on the open sea." He looked at her sideways. "Tell me, Lady Aranati, do you have a romantic attachment to the pirate?"

She froze at the question. Did she even know the answer? They had parted on such bad terms and she had no idea of his true feelings. Could she be frank with the admiral or would that be a mistake? "No, Admiral. Do you have an attachment to Samael Delacost? He's your brother after all. I'd imagine that would be important to you."

He walked away from her, shaking his head. "He stands for everything I hate; he's a thief and has no respect for authority. Focusing on that is the only way I can do my job, for I may be taking my own kin back to face death."

Her heart beat fast. "You could do that?"

"It is he not I who has made this choice. He has lived the life of a pirate and has caused the death of sailors. I can't let that go unpunished. The king won't allow it."

"And of course, the king doesn't yet know of your relationship to Delacost?"

"And will not if I have my way." He met Esta's gaze. "You'll say nothing to anyone about my link to the pirate."

"You can't even say his name," she breathed.

"Tell me you'll keep my secret," Nikolas snapped.

She drew in a deep breath. "I'll keep your secret, Admiral, but you're making a mistake sacrificing Samael for your career. There's good in him and he hasn't had your privileges. Think on that before you toss him to the sharks." She turned and left the cabin, hurrying up the passageway and the ladder that took her topside. The open air and fresh breeze banished the feeling she had below decks - that the walls were closing in. Would there be anything she could do to save Samael? If his own brother wouldn't acknowledge him, what could she do?

Nikolas was much tougher than Esta had envisaged when she advised Samael to tell the admiral of their common mother. He was having trouble coming to grips with an older brother and struggling to hold onto the life and reality he had known. Could she convince him to save his brother rather than condemn him?

She knew in her heart there was good in the man who called himself the Singing Pirate. But was there enough virtue to enable him to be saved?

CHAPTER 18

ESTA'S body vibrated with a fine tension she couldn't banish, as the admiral's ship slid between the walls of the channel. This could spell disaster for them all. She could imagine them smashed against the rocks and taking on water; more real after the recent experience of the loss of her own ship. Samael had to be here, or she didn't know if she had the stomach for more searching, more danger.

Katrine was high in the mast, straining for the first look into the harbor - a vulnerable position should they hit the rock wall. But her sister couldn't be dissuaded from the task. Nikolas had to wonder how a lady came to be so comfortable high up in a ship's main top castle. He appeared to admire Katrine for having such courage, but Esta worried about her. It could go so very wrong.

A shout from above had her looking aloft. Katrine waved and gave a thumbs up - the sign their quarry was present. Nikolas waved to her from his position at the wheel. Another shout from the starboard watch heralded a narrowing of the margin between the hull and the rocks. Nikolas corrected and the unmistakable low grinding of wood on rock shuddered through Esta. It was short-lived and she heaved a sigh of relief until another sailor yelled from the port side. Nikolas spun the wheel but not in time to avoid an even longer brush with the rocks.

She tried to block out Nikolas's muttering and swearing. Perhaps the ship's hull was too broad to fit up this channel. She glanced above to see Katrine clinging to the mast for dear life.

Another two scrapes with the rocks had her gripping the rail, knuckles white and her breath coming in gasps. She wished they had rowed up the inlet, leaving both ships outside, but that might have been just as foolhardy.

"It widens a little up ahead," Katrine called.

Esta craned her neck but there was naught to see from her position. She hoped it opened out under water too. *Foolish!* Nikolas must want Samael very badly to take this risk for himself, his people and the ship. That didn't bode well for Samael's future.

* * *

Sam paced up and down the strip of beach in front of his hut, cursing himself for being complacent. His scouts had seen the approach of the naval ships and he assumed they would pass by. He couldn't have done anything anyway. *Silver Lady* lay at anchor in the middle of the harbor and there'd be no escape for her until the tide ran out in four hours or so.

He knew who'd be on the vessel that negotiated the channel.

Nikolas Cosara. No one else would risk life and limb to track him down. It looked like he'd have his showdown and soon. But how to play this? He could take everyone into the hills and forests and hide for many months, living on the land until Nikolas gave up. But he'd lose his ship. He had no doubt Nikolas would take *Silver Lady* for his own. He might even be stranded here on this island. Eventually they'd be rescued but he had no yearning for the life of a castaway.

On balance, he had decided to fight here on the sand. His *Lenweri* were hidden in trees and behind dunes, ready with their arrows, knives and swords. They had vowed to defend him when the admiral entered the channel. But he'd find a way to save them even if it meant running away.

Damn the man! Why couldn't Cosara leave him be. He wasn't doing much harm. He thought of the men who had died recently and cursed again. He hadn't meant for anyone to get hurt, knowing it would draw unwelcome attention.

He raised his scope at the channel and a ship's masts appeared above the cliffs, a figure in the castle. Someone with…long dark hair! *Lady Star!* It must be her. And if Lady Star was on that ship then Esta would be too. His gut clenched at the thought. There'd be no fighting on this beach; none at all. He couldn't risk her being hurt no matter the risk to his own liberty.

As the ship slid along the channel, she sawed from side to side. It had to be a hairy ride in the main top castle. Lady Star held on grimly, her hands clenching the rail. He could barely breathe watching her. One wrong move by the captain and …

He swung the scope down as the ship popped into the harbor, searching for the woman he knew would be on deck. There she was, standing in the bow, her feet apart, riding the waves as if she'd been born on a ship. Her chestnut hair was secured with a scarf and she was dressed in breeches and tunic. He couldn't take his eyes from her. That tunic fit so snugly it must have been tailor-made. He licked his lips as he imagined running his hands over those curves.

He realized where his thoughts had taken him and turned on his heel. "Nande!"

The elf materialized almost in front of him and Sam clamped his teeth on a curse. "Lady Moonlight is on that ship with the admiral. There'll be no fighting this day."

Nande stared. "We are to surrender? Sorry, Captain, but I have no wish to be imprisoned or worse. You have seen the troubles between my people and the Thorians."

"Yes, yes," he said. "Damn it Nande, I know our peoples are virtually at war, but I have no choice. I can't put those women at risk."

"So, you choose this woman over *Lenweri* who have endangered their lives for you time and again?"

"Yes, I do, and you've sworn to obey me." This could be disaster if Nande pushed it. Sam had no real idea how far his authority went with the elves or even how far Nande's power extended. They were odd people at times.

Nande was silent for a long time as the ship drew closer, his face devoid of expression. "You swore to protect us and that is what I expect you to do. I will not have my people imprisoned."

He sighed. "I don't know if I can protect you. You're pirates just as I am. You've killed, stolen. The king will see you as criminals."

Nande folded his arms over his chest. "You will protect us, or you will never field a *Lenweri* crew in future."

"It will be as you say," Sam said.

Fine situation it was. The pirate captain dealing with a mutiny at this most perilous time. Not to mention his mutinous heart that pounded at seeing Esta. He turned to watch as the admiral's ship weighed anchor and several rowboats were lowered over the side.

* * *

He was as splendid as she remembered. His light brown hair had grown longer, but he was the same man who had twice saved her life and then turned his back. Hands on narrow hips he watched as they rowed toward him, his elven crew spread out behind. Esta's hands gripped the sides of the boat so tightly she couldn't feel her fingers.

Nikolas had asked her to allow him to handle the confrontation but how could she do that? She knew Samael better than anyone here and Nikolas knew him not at all. The boat's bottom scraped the sand and sailors leaped into the shallows to draw it up the beach. She and Katrine were helped out and now Esta was close enough to see his eyes. They burned through her leaving her shivering. He was angry, trapped, perhaps even a little frightened. This magnificent man would lose his freedom, she was sure. She couldn't bear to think of him in a cell or at the end of a noose.

Nikolas stalked past her and Katrine and stopped several paces away from his brother.

"Hello, Brother," Samael said, a smirk on his lips. Some *Lenweri* were close enough to hear and looked at each other. A few muttered. "Welcome to my hideaway."

"Cut the crap, Delacost," Nikolas said, his jaw so tight Esta wondered that he could even speak. "You are under arrest and your crew with you. I charge you with theft and murder on the high seas and warn that anything you say can be held against you."

Samael held out his hands. "Bind me and take me but leave my crew alone. They were following my orders."

Nikolas frowned. "We both know that won't wash with the king."

"I've put up no resistance," Samael said. "Surely that counts in my favor?" His eyes flicked to Esta and he inclined his head. "Lady Aranati, I suppose I have you to thank that they found me." His voice was so bitter her heart broke.

She swallowed a lump in her throat. "I wanted to help," she said. "The admiral would have found you sooner or later."

"I was hoping for later," Samael said.

He stepped closer to Nikolas. Esta hurried forward until her body was between the two men.

"Don't make this harder than it has to be, Samael," she said, her hand on his chest.

"I merely wished to ask if blood means nothing," he said. "We have shared blood, Admiral. You need me."

"I need you like a hole in the head," Nikolas ground out. "I was doing just fine and now you show up with your swashbuckling ways and elven crew…You're an embarrassment, and worse than that, you're a killer."

"Wait, Nikolas," he said. "I'm sorry. I didn't mean for anyone to die. I tried to take the ships by surprise, while most slept."

Esta cleared her throat, thinking of Stino and his death at the hands of the *Lenweri*. She frowned at him, even though he had evened the ledger by saving her twice since. He had the grace to look embarrassed.

"We can cut a deal, Nikolas," he said.

"Don't call me that! You don't have the right to call me that!" He walked up the beach and Samael watched him go, a look of longing on his face. He wanted a brother, that much was clear, not only to save his skin but to love.

Esta was afraid he'd be disappointed. Nikolas didn't need a brother. He had a wife, cousins, friends and a good life. He had everything while Samael might be losing everything.

As she stared at Nikolas, Samael spoke to her. "Of all the people who might come looking for me, I never imagined you."

"Well, you don't know me very well then," she said, her gaze meeting his. "I thought I might be able to stop Nikolas from snapping your stupid neck, but you see it as a betrayal. I never meant it that way."

"Difficult to see it any other way from where I stand."

She looked into his eyes and her heart ached at his distress. She must make him understand! "I gave up everything to come and find you."

"What did you give up? Drudgery? You love the sea. This was no chore."

Katrine hissed. "She gave up a friendship and a marriage, idiot. She was betrothed, the wedding scheduled for this very day. Her man will likely never speak to her again and what will become of the estate I don't know."

"Katrine!" Esta said. "This is my fight."

Samael stared. "Your betrothed? That was mighty sudden. You couldn't wait to land some poor sod who'd bail you out of trouble."

"How dare you?" She snapped, furious that he should dismiss her sacrifice. She pulled her anger back under control; reminded herself it would not help to fly at him and scratch his eyes out. She would not allow him to bait her into disgracing herself. "I'm not getting any younger. Reid is a widower, a master goldsmith who is lonely and in need of family. I'm young enough to give him that and he could provide security. Do you begrudge me that, knowing how hard I've worked to keep the estate afloat?"

"I'm disappointed you thought you could settle for a marriage of convenience," he said, his voice softer and eyes sadder than ever. "It's beneath you."

"Well, I don't care what you think. It doesn't matter now anyway. Reid won't want me after I left him to sail in search of you. What man could forgive that?"

"Some men might admire your passion and daring," he said, the intensity of his gaze heating her blood.

She was so distracted by him that she forgot her question, forgot she might be required to reply. Katrine nudged her. "Ah… I'd be optimistic indeed to think that Reid could see my actions as anything but a rejection"

"And have you rejected him?"

She had asked herself the same question over and over. If she returned and Reid would still have her, would she go through with the marriage? It wouldn't be fair to him if she was unable to commit herself. Luckily, she didn't have to answer that question.

Nikolas re-joined them, the tension between the two men palpable. Their profiles were very similar, just with slightly different coloring and Nikolas the bigger of the two. She wondered how this would all end.

"Have you come to a decision, Admiral?" Samael asked, his arms crossed, and feet planted in the sand.

"I can't overlook your crimes, Delacost, no matter the blood that links us. You must return with me to Wildecoast and answer for your actions. Your crew must also return."

There was angry muttering from the *Lenweri*, and many raised their weapons.

"Leave the *Lenweri* and I swear I'll come in peace and allow whatever judgments you require," Samael said.

Nikolas's eyes flickered to the elves and back to Samael. "I can't do that, man. After the trouble we are having with this race within Thorius, there's no way I can pardon your crew. If I try, the king will overturn my order and send me to detain them. I'll see you all get a fair trial but that's all I can promise."

"That's no promise," Samael snapped. "I swore I'd protect them only moments ago and now I must go back on my word. You'll regret this, Cosara."

"Your threats are meaningless—"

An arrow flew past Esta and the next thing she knew, Samael charged at her and Katrine, lifted them both off the ground and ran with them under his arms, one on each side.

Esta shrieked and pounded at his side. "Put me down. What are you doing?"

"Saving your life, Lady," he said, his breath coming hard and fast as they neared the beached boats. "Get in and keep your heads down." When they were in, he pushed the boat out into the shallows and handed them knives.

Esta brandished two of her own. "Keep your weapons, you may need them." She sent him a look that she hoped said everything she felt for him. He gave their boat a last push and waded back to shore and the chaos that reined.

Kingdom sailors fought the *Lenweri* and Samael cursed and ran back toward the melee. The elves had downed bows and taken up swords. Nikolas was fending off three elves as Samael joined him. She was sure one of the elves was Nande. She held her breath, wondering who her pirate would help. Samael smashed the butt of his sword against Nande's temple. The *Lenweri* leader dropped to the sand unmoving and Samael engaged one of the other two elves. He and Nikolas fought side by side, dispatching the elves and turning as one to clash with the rear of a pack of *Lenweri* intent on reaching the water.

She wished she could understand what Samael was saying. He shouted at the elves, his former crew, in their language, but all it seemed to do was increase the ferocity of their attack.

"Can't you do something?" she asked Katrine. "I'm sure he'll be hurt."

"I would if I could be sure of hitting the elves and not our men," Katrine said. "They fight like demons these *Lenweri*. Surely they have some loyalty to Samael?"

"It appears not. There must have been a captain's pledge given and now he has been unable to keep it, they've taken matters into their own hands." *Her* hands were curled into fists as she watched the fight sweep back and forth along the beach. Elves and men were dropping and not getting up, some moaned and others were still. The casualties looked even.

"Who'll be left to sail the ships away from this place?" At least she had no fear that she and Katrine would be safe, but would they be able to leave this deserted island?

"Don't fear, Sister," Katrine said. "I'm quite able to defend us no matter who is the victor."

"You forget we must have enough crew to sail. At the moment it looks unlikely." Esta chewed on her lower lip as she lost sight of Samael. The brothers had been separated and now battled on opposite sides of the beach. "Go to him," she said to herself. As if he heard her words, Nikolas extracted himself and battled his way over to his brother until they fought back to back.

A group of a dozen elves broke away and bolted toward the boats. Some peeled off and headed for Esta and Katrine. Esta pulled her knives while Katrine muttered an incantation. She let fly a fireball that smashed into the leading elves, then turned and sent another to the shore.

"Don't fire the boats!" Esta screamed.

There was terrible carnage as the fireballs hit elven bodies and they ran screaming into the sea. One boat was set afire, but the remainder had escaped damage so far. And then six *Lenweri* appeared beside their boat, standing in thigh-deep water, their oval irises coldly strange. They piled into the boat and while Katrine fought them like a demon, Esta held two at bay in the prow of the boat, brandishing her knives at their faces. The remaining two elves grabbed the oars and began rowing toward the ships.

The movement of the boat took Esta's attention for a split second. That was enough for her two assailants to wrench the knives from her hands. She was pushed hard into the bottom of the vessel. She screamed as one of the elves hit Katrine's temple with the butt of his knife.

"That will tame the witch," the *Lenweri* said. It was an elf Esta could remember sharing an ale with on board *Silver Lady*. She watched desperately for signs of life from her sister, her gut churning.

"Don't hurt her," she said, a sob escaping. "Please."

"She wouldn't hesitate to hurt us," the *Lenweri* said. "Blindfold and gag her."

Esta tried to see what was happening on the beach but she was surrounded by wet *Lenweri* bodies. This had gone so very wrong.

Where is Sam?

And suddenly he was there, his head above the side of the boat, water cascading off his hair and shoulders. He shook the water from his eyes and punched her captor in the side of the head. The *Lenweri* tumbled into the three elves guarding Katrine. Esta pulled a knife from her boot and stabbed the elf standing on her other side. As Sam heaved himself aboard, she stood and kicked the Lenweri in front of her in the head. He reeled back and tumbled over the side. Sam set about dispatching the other three until they were alone on the boat. He slumped in the bottom, gasping for breath, his eyes closed.

"Sam," she said, falling to her knees beside him. "What's amiss?" And then she took in the many cuts over his body and the blood leeching in ever growing pools.

"I'll live," he said, eyes still closed. "Check your sister."

She had seen the even rise and fall of Katrine's chest before Sam's advent but she crawled over to her sister and probed the nasty bruise on her temple. There didn't seem any broken skull bones, but neither was there any sign her sister would soon awake.

"Katrine, can you hear me? If you can, squeeze my hand." There was the faintest tightening of the cold fingers that lay in hers. Esta let out a long breath. "She'll be well, I think."

She turned back to Sam who appeared to be fading fast. "Sam, can you hear me?"

She shook his shoulders, but he had sagged against the side of the boat, his eyes closed and his breath fast and shallow. Esta turned to the beach where the few remaining elves had been herded into a huddle, guarded by Nikolas Cosara and seven of his men. She sat, grabbed the oars and started rowing, slow regular strokes when everything within screamed at her to go faster. But faster would only upset her rhythm and slow her down.

As she neared the beach, Nikolas waded out to her and dragged the little boat up on the sand.

"How is he?" he asked, a telling statement when Katrine lay unmoving as well.

"I think he's dying. He has lost so much blood."

Nikolas stepped into the boat and hauled his brother over his shoulders then carried him up the beach, laying him on a stack of sail cloth. He removed his shirt and started tearing it into bandages and wrapping Sam's hurts to stem the blood flow.

"You're right," Nikolas said. "He's close to death."

"Then save him, Admiral," she snapped, helping Katrine out of the boat and up the beach to join them. "You can't let him die."

Nikolas's eyes fluttered closed and he let out a long sigh, crouched next to his brother, his hands keeping pressure on the more serious wounds until the seepage of blood slowed. After observing for long moments, he nodded and stood, walking to the huts nearby. He returned with blankets for the two patients.

She collected wood for a fire and soon had a good blaze going and water heating in a pot. He needed fluid and warmth and perhaps he'd live. In a daze, she raided the huts and found enough food to make a broth which she fed to Sam and Katrine. Esta had some herself for she'd never been so cold or scared in the warm light of day.

The sailors tied up the able bodied *Lenweri* and set about making themselves a meal and treating their wounded. Then they buried the dead - a huge task. Nikolas watched with bleak eyes even though he was the victor.

"Cheer up, Admiral," she said. "You'll have your day in court."

He turned and glared at her. "I can't stand the loss of life. I had planned on taking my men back to their wives and children and instead…" His voice broke on the words and Esta realized he was distraught. "And my brother lies here, fighting for life." He looked away. "Why is it that everyone I care for I lose?"

"He's still alive. All is not lost."

Nikolas cleared his throat and wiped his eyes. "It's time we looked at those wounds. I take it you're acquainted with a needle and thread?"

She stared at the admiral, wondering at the depths he had revealed. Was there hope for a relationship between him and Sam?

She stood and brought a pot of water she had boiled and allowed to cool. There were special herbs in the water that would aid healing and stop wounds going foul. She was no wise woman, but she'd seen her share of illness and injury both on the land and at sea and Katrine had taught her basic herb lore.

While Nikolas stripped Sam of his shirt and breeches, she removed the bandages one by one. Mindful of the admiral's eye upon her, she cleaned the wounds with quick efficient sweeps of her cloth when her fingers itched to stroke the firm muscles of his chest. She stitched the deepest wounds and they found clean shirts in one of the huts and tore them up for fresh bandages.

Sam's breathing had deepened and slowed which she knew was a good sign. He wasn't feverish and rested quietly. His hands and feet were cold though and that scared her.

"You can't leave me, pirate," she said under her breath. "I've given up everything for you."

CHAPTER 19

S AM wandered in a place of darkness but there was light ahead. He wanted to walk toward it, but something kept him anchored. There was a voice, a familiar voice, filled with fear. Gentle hands traced his skin; then there was pain. His head pounded and he knew if he could reach that light, the pain would end. Paradise might await there. He could stand some paradise right about now.

As he strained to break the bonds that tied him, that voice distracted, speaking of real things like wounds and bandages, telling him he couldn't leave.

He had a feeling he owed her nothing, had given over and over; only to find she had betrayed him. But their friendship was ever tenuous, more a rivalry than a true relationship. What they shared was primal; what her hands promised was gentle and loving, and he was sure he didn't understand those conditions.

His spirit drew away from the light and slid down a dark tunnel. The decision had been made for him, perhaps by his traitorous body that would never give up. He was going back, to the voice, to the pain and to a woman who didn't know she needed him.

The pain mounted, in his head and all over his body. He gasped and sat up, the movement blackening his vision. As the blindness faded, she came into view - anxious, beautiful and tentative. He tried to smile but knew it was more a grimace.

"Lady," he croaked, and lay back down. He turned his head and found his brother. "Admiral."

Nikolas nodded, as grim as ever. Did the man never smile? "You had better call me Nikolas, at least in private. What we've endured, well, it makes a difference."

"Even though you're here because of me?"

"You could have chosen to fight with your men, instead you decided to save the women and fight with us. It tells me you're not beyond redemption."

Sam nodded and the movement sent a spear of pure pain through his skull. "It could be too soon to judge that." He looked at Esta but didn't know what to say.

"I want to thank you," she said. "By now we could have been on the ocean, captive of elves and the Goddess only knows what would've happened."

"I know what you did, Lady Aranati. You tended me, brought me back from the brink. I don't know if you did me a favor. At least dead I'd be spared the noose and might even have had a song or two composed about my death."

She gasped. "You ungrateful …bastard! You're wrong anyway. Somehow you would've lived. A man like you is not so easy to kill." Her voice failed on the last words.

Nikolas cleared his throat. "I should go and check on my men." He walked away, leaving an awkward silence.

"How do you expect me to react to your actions?" Sam said, the rage in his voice diminished by pain. "You helped Nikolas find me. I was perfectly happy roaming the seas, never to set eyes on you or my brother."

"I don't think you were happy. Your raids were becoming violent. Nikolas had to act, and I came along to make sure you were safe. I thought maybe I could save you from yourself."

He frowned. "Instead you nearly got taken hostage."

"Don't you see?" she said. "I couldn't bear not knowing what was happening to you. I feared for you, Sam. I have deep feelings a betrothed woman shouldn't have. I have them all the same." She took a deep breath and her heart steadied. "I think I love you."

He barked out a harsh laugh. "You think! Always so cautious, Lady." He levered himself up, so he sat facing her. "When are you going to let your heart free? Well I *do* love you. Despite your betrayal, despite our different stations, despite your infuriating control issues, even though you always pull away first - I love you."

* * *

Esta's mouth dropped open and she blinked away tears that tried to steal the moment. She wouldn't cry, she'd be strong and clear and forthright. She blew out the breath she'd been holding.

"I…ah…you stir me as no man ever has. I wake up thinking of you and go to bed in the same condition. I imagine what you might be doing, saying, what trouble you might be in, wonder if you're still alive. I can't stand being apart from you any longer. I've fought and denied; this is where it has led me. Is that love?"

He smiled and her heart melted. A surge of…love…lifted her up and drove her toward him, the man who had saved her life, the one she had chosen over her betrothed. She leaned further forward and laid her lips on his, tasted the salty essence of him, pushed her hands up into his hair. His mouth moved beneath hers and his arms enfolded her; the passion that ignited between them could have melted the sand beneath.

Esta lost all sense of time and place, let her body free for once, just once, to see what would happen. It wasn't a conscious thought, but a response to him, to the fact that he was alive, and for this moment, he was hers. He groaned and she pulled back, thinking she'd hurt him. What she saw in his eyes was anything but hurt. It was pure desire and burning bright. She dived back in, pressing close, noting him stir beneath her. She wanted more, wanted everything that was possible between a man and woman. Everything that couldn't happen here.

This time when she drew back, the cold light of reality had doused the fire in his eyes.

"We can't do this here, Esta," he said.

"Well," Katrine said from beside them. "That's a relief. I was wondering when you two would come to your senses. Everyone is watching."

Sam looked around but Esta couldn't bring herself to see what would be on their faces - disgust, pity, amusement? They saw her as a fool, she knew. A fool who had fallen in love with a pirate, a man who might have no future.

"It has happened again, hasn't it," he asked. "I can see all the doubt resurface. You're telling yourself this—", he gestured between them, "can never be."

"And what are you saying? That all is well? That we can go home and be married and live happily ever after?"

He snorted a laugh that held no mirth. "Of course, it won't be simple, perhaps not even possible, but I want you to let yourself go, or you'll kill whatever time we might have."

"I don't know if I can do that."

"Try, Esta. We're in love. We're still breathing by the grace of the Goddess. We've helped each other through more trials than I care to remember. Just let it be."

Tears welled but she took his hands and nodded. She'd try, she really would.

* * *

The voyage back was heaven and hell. Sam's admiration for and dependence on Esta grew daily. They'd spent whatever time together they could, but there had been little privacy. She had tended his wounds and they healed. But he feared it was all coming to an end. The days of learning about and exploring each other's bodies was sweet torture. Now they sat together at dusk in a sheltered part of the bow and toasted their love over a sunset meal.

"It's so beautiful on the ocean," she said. "I could never live away from the sea for long. Losing *Sea Sprite* was like losing part of me."

"I'll find you another *Sea Sprite* one day, love, and she'll be fleeter and grander than your old vessel." He reached for her hand and squeezed it.

She gazed at the horizon. "It won't be the same. She was a link with my father who taught me to sail." She frowned. "But that's in the past and we have larger concerns."

"Ever the pragmatist," he said, smiling. "You're allowed to mourn you know. Do you fear if you sit still and live for a moment, something will catch up with you?"

She looked at him, eyes narrowed. "How well you understand me. That's exactly how I feel, but I never know if I'm running away from something or chasing it."

"Perhaps a little of both." He raised her hand to his lips and kissed it. "I so wish we could be together, truly together."

"I have to believe that Nikolas has a plan," she said, "even though he has studiously avoided us for the entire voyage."

"He has much on his mind and I'm sure the thought of how he'll deal with me is a large part of that. I feel a little sorry for him."

"How so?" she asked.

"It has been a shock to discover his older brother and to learn that same man is everything he never wanted in a sibling."

Esta put her glass and plate to the side and crawled over. Her lips met his and he forgot what he'd been saying. Her mouth was sweet, but her kisses were always laced with a restraint, sadness, as though she waited for a dark cloud to rain on her love. Perhaps he was the same. And then there was the ever-present crew and Katrine. They were hardly the right conditions to express one's passion.

Despite the melancholy, passion grew between them until he was breathing hard. His fingers cradled her face and threaded up through her beautiful chestnut hair. When he thought of all she had sacrificed to come and find him, it took his breath away. Right then, he wanted her so much he ached all over.

He pulled her against him, and they reclined on a roll of sail. Drawing her cloak over them both, he returned to his exploration of her lips. She responded and he allowed his hand to drift down over the side of her breast, bringing a sharp breath from his lady.

"Sam, we can't."

"Hush," he said. "No one will know."

"Everyone will know."

"And do you care?" He imagined her throat tightening in the darkness for her reply was strained.

"I should, but I don't."

She had changed a lot, this lady who had bested him on the high seas all those weeks ago. He liked to think he had changed her, freed her just a little from the chains of her life. He allowed his hand to slide over her waist and down to cup her sex which was sealed away by her breeches. *Damned breeches*! There was a good reason women didn't wear them and this was it! He longed to take her and make love to her for the first time. But she deserved better. Esta deserved a soft bed, romantic lighting and a man who didn't have a sentence of death hanging over him. He could feel her wet all the way through those breeches and he groaned.

She moved, her hands between them and Sam thought she must be removing her pants. He stilled her hands.

"Stop, love," he said. "I can't take you here, you deserve better."

She laughed, a light sound on a dark night. "It was you I was thinking of, Sam. I believe men enjoy what I had in mind." Her hands moved, and he realized she was unlacing his breeches. His heart pounded. Would she really do that?

He didn't have long to wait as warm, wet lips encased his rod and he had to stop from leaping right off the deck. He bit down on his lower lip to stop the groan that rose up. She cupped his balls and stroked the base of his dick while sucking on the head. When he thought it couldn't get any better, her probing tongue entered his tip, sending shocks through him.

He clutched her arms and struggled for words. "Esta," he croaked. "Stop."

She looked up at him, and he could just make out the whites of her eyes in the gloom. "Is this not enjoyable?"

He huffed out a breath. "Too good. If you continue, I'll come, and you might not like that."

Her lips encased him once more and she moaned, the vibrations setting off tremors in his rod. Damn it, he couldn't hold back. He thrust into her mouth and she clamped her lips over her teeth and sucked hard. It was only seconds before he lost himself in her warmth. Her body tensed but she remained where she was, accepting him, all of him.

As the moment passed, Sam took several long deep breaths to slow his racing heart. "That was wonderful."

Esta lay on his lap, her arms around his waist. "I'm glad I could give you pleasure."

"Was it very awful?" he asked. "Me coming in your mouth?"

"I wondered how it would taste. I'd do it again so don't fear you've disgusted me. I'd do anything for you, Samael Delacost."

"I'm beginning to see that," he said, rubbing her back. "I'm sorry I ever doubted you, ever thought you had any other agenda but love when you came in search of me."

"Don't you ever forget it, pirate."

He drew in a deep breath and pulled her close. He wished it could always be like this - just the two of them. But that was never going to be the case. Tomorrow he'd face the justice of the kingdom and there'd be jail; or worse. He couldn't regret any decision he'd made. There was no point. He and Esta would be together or they would not. Regret wouldn't change anything. He covered himself and lay with her until the horizon began to show the first faint rays of the sun.

CHAPTER 20

ESTA left Sam at dawn and went to her cabin to change. She found Katrine in bed staring at the ceiling.

"I wondered where you were." Katrine fixed her with that look that had become even more potent with the changes in her eye color. She was one of the few people Katrine looked directly at anymore.

"I needed time with him." Her heart ached at the thought of being separated. He was so tender with her and her love for him was so much more than anything she had ever felt for Reid.

Katrine shook her head. "You had it all and you had to go and ruin it for a pirate. Not only that, for a pirate who'll either rot in jail or hang."

"When you say it like that, it sounds hopeless," she said.

"It *is* hopeless. Even Nikolas won't be able to save him. That's if he even wants to."

"I have to believe he will come out of this. If I didn't, I'd shrivel and die."

Katrine got up from the bed and confronted her sister. "I hate to see you do this. You deserve happiness and all you'll have is despair with Delacost. When we dock, you must go to Reid and beg for his mercy."

Esta stared. "No." As she said the word, she realized she'd never ask Reid to take her back. "He's too good a man for me to ask that. I've ruined what we had, and it would forever taint us. Let him start afresh with another."

Katrine snorted. "Perhaps I'll ask him to take me as wife. Perhaps he's the man to overlook my faults and keep me safe."

She shook her head and grabbed her sister's upper arms. "Stop it, now. You will *not* do that. Any man would be lucky to have you as wife. You'll get through this difficult time and learn there is love for you yet."

"So, I'm not to settle as you were willing to do?"

"I was wrong, and the first test of my feelings showed me that. I went running to Sam. He is where my heart lies, and I have to believe he will be given to me in the end."

Katrine studied her sister's face. "You truly believe that!"

"I've been on a journey to find my heart and in Sam I've done that. I don't care that he's a pirate. I too have sunk low because I had no choice. I have no right to judge him. He has a core of good that will see him safe. Nikolas has seen it and will do everything he can to pull his brother from this mess."

Katrine's eyes widened. "I think you're more insane than I."

She laid her hand along her sister's cheek. "You're not insane. You'll find your feet. Just don't give up."

Katrine closed her eyes and let her head drop. "I can't see the way forward. Not since the crystal cave. It burnt the life out of me and what's left scares me at times. I find myself wishing for solitude, hating myself for wishing that. Hetty helped but only I can truly heal myself. I don't know if I have the energy."

Esta pulled her sister into her arms. "Please don't give up. I love you and want you to be happy. You have so much to give, including love. Also, I need you Katrine, now more than ever before. And mother needs you."

"I'll try for you and for mother." She smiled but Esta saw it was for show, to reassure, and she wasn't comforted. Katrine would need to be watched and cared for if she was to navigate her way through this.

* * *

Sam sailed into Wildecoast harbor with dread in his heart. Even from the heads he could see a sizeable welcoming committee. It seemed they had been spotted well before now. Three returning ships, instead of the two that had left, eloquently announced the triumph of Nikolas's mission.

Esta was still below decks and Sam hoped he'd have a quiet word with her before he went to his fate. He tried to concentrate on the happy times in his life, the love he had for his parents, the joy he'd found on the sea, his brief soaring love with Esta and the chance to know Nikolas.

He discovered a large part of those happy times were in relationships - that shocked him. Before Esta, before Nikolas, that wouldn't have been the case.

Nikolas hadn't revealed what he would do when they docked, and Sam surmised that was because he couldn't predict what pressure the king would place on him. Men had died because of Sam's actions, even if he had never wished for it. He had to pay. He hoped his actions back on the island had redeemed him somewhat, but would that count for enough with the king? No, Nikolas had made him no promises.

He became aware of someone behind him and turned to find his love, tears in her eyes. He clenched his jaw, desperate to take her in his arms and never let her go. "Have faith, love," he said. "I'll come through this if it's possible."

"I'm trying but the thought of you in prison keeps pushing at me. I can't lose you."

He took her hand and raised it to his lips. "Happy thoughts. Remember what we share. Don't let anything else in."

She nodded, perhaps unsure of her voice.

Sam turned back to the rail and they stood side by side, not touching, but one in heart and soul.

As the ships docked, he watched his *Silver Lady* as Nikolas's men tied her up beside them. He missed her already. The Goddess only knew when he'd see her next. She had been seized as proceeds of crime and Nikolas would likely draft her into his navy. *Storm Chaser* was at risk too if he ever discovered Sam's other ship.

He touched Esta's skirt and she turned to him. "Love, you must have *Storm Chaser*. She's now called *Dawn Lady* and lies at anchor in Shawmere. I should've given her to you when you lost *Sea Sprite*. Remember me when you sail in her."

"I'll accept but only until you can captain her."

"Until then. Find Willem Septo, the harbor master in Shawmere. Tell him Samael Delacost sent you to claim *Dawn Lady*. When he asks for the word, tell him 'Vitavia'. He'll know I sent you."

"I'll do as you say, but not until I know the outcome of your trial."

"It's your decision, love, but I feel better knowing *Dawn Lady* is in good hands."

Nikolas approached with two sailors. "I'm sorry, Delacost. I must have you secured for entry into Wildecoast."

Sam met his brother's eyes and for a moment was seized by the need to flee - he was close enough to the side to leap to the wharf then into the harbor and swim for dear life. He might have half a chance.

"Don't do anything stupid, man." Nikolas said. The sailors gripped his arms while Nikolas placed the manacles on his wrists and ankles.

Just like that, all chance of escape was gone. He glanced at Esta. Her eyes were wide and shimmered with tears. She turned away without a word. She'd not watch him in his disgrace then.

He battled for composure as he walked with Nikolas and the sailors down the gangway and along the wharf to the dock. Shuffled would've been a more accurate description. Shame curled up through his gut and dragged his eyes to the timber beneath his feet. He was better than this, deserved more, but this was the hand life had dealt. And so, he gritted his teeth, put one boot in front of the other and raised his eyes to the crowd that grew closer. There were few friendly faces to be seen.

Soldiers on the docks had to clear a path but even so, Sam was jostled and spat on. Threats to his person washed over him. All it would take was one well-aimed knife or arrow and he might breathe his last. He didn't want to die like this - scum crushed under the feet of the masses.

A carriage appeared ahead, and the jostling and jeers rose in intensity.

"Head for the coach." Nikolas pushed in front of Sam, forging a path and perhaps protecting his brother, risking his own safety. Nikolas reached the carriage and wrenched the door open. He turned and pulled Sam close, then shoved him into the vehicle, jumping in behind.

Sam took a seat opposite a dark-haired man who looked at him with unveiled hostility.

"Kain." Nikolas gripped the man's hand and engulfed him in a brief hug before sitting beside him. "You always know just when I need you."

"Happy coincidence," the other man said. "Alique and I were in Wildecoast and I happened to hear you were on your way in. I predicted there'd be trouble so brought the coach down."

"Well, I couldn't be happier to see anyone."

"Except for Merielle, of course," their rescuer said.

"Indeed, is she at the castle?

"Been there ever since you left, I hear."

Sam cleared his throat. "Admiral, will Lady Aranati and her sister be safe?"

The other man's dark gaze snapped to his. "What concern are the nobility to you, pirate?"

Nikolas placed a hand on his friend's arm. "Peace, Kain. Delacost's concern for the ladies is true." He looked at Sam. "I left instructions for them to wait until the crowd dispersed. I'll have a coach sent for them as soon as I can. In the meantime, the wharf is sealed."

Sam nodded, still concerned for Esta. She'd been through enough on his behalf.

"This is Kain Jazara," Nikolas said, "once army general of Wildecoast, now aide to the king. Kain, this is Samael Delacost."

Sam nodded at Jazara and got naught but scorn in return. He'd heard of the half-cast elf who had fallen from favor when it was revealed his father was an elven king. The man could hardly treat Sam with disdain when he had such a murky past.

"Where will you take me, Admiral?" Sam asked.

"You'll be taken to the prison and held until your trial is over. I want you to know I'll speak on your behalf to King Beniel and tell him of your deeds at the end."

"What deeds?" Jazara snapped.

"I'll tell you later. Suffice to say, things could've been ugly if Delacost hadn't thrown his lot in with us. His crew mutinied."

"My *Lenweri* crew, Jazara," Sam said.

Jazara's eyes narrowed. "You had an elven crew?"

He nodded. "They're hellish good at night as you would know." He watched Kain's throat bob up and down. What had rattled him so much?

"Are there survivors of this crew?" Jazara asked. "I'd like to speak with them."

"I thought as much," Nikolas said. "There are a handful of survivors, but I doubt you'll get much from them. I'll see you get a chance before they're put to death."

His heart gave a great thud. Nande would soon die and there was no hope of Sam intervening. He was responsible, even though the elf had turned on him at the end. Old habits…

"As I assume their captain will face death for his actions." Kain Jazara fixed Sam with a stare that held no mercy. "Have we met?"

"I assure you I've never crossed your path, Sir." He was fast developing a dislike for the arrogant aide. "But there's a reason I might seem familiar."

"Never mind, Delacost," Nikolas said. "I'll tell Kain later. You need to keep your mouth shut. Like we discussed."

Sam went cold. Could his own brother betray him? Would he hide their relationship, so he came out smelling of roses while Sam spent the rest of his life in a dungeon? "You better take great care, Admiral. Unless you send your lackey to slit my throat one night, I'll not stay silent forever."

"What the blast is he raving about, Niko?" Jazara asked.

"I said I'd tell you later. Let me get him bedded down and I'll meet with you."

Sam's gut churned. He had no control over events now; was like a piece of driftwood on the ocean. The Wildecoast currents would swirl around him and he'd have no influence. He had to depend on Nikolas and Esta to see him through this. In his world, trust was a scarce commodity. He knew he could depend on Esta, but what of Nikolas?

CHAPTER 21

ESTA entered her chambers to find Merielle reclining in her sitting room. Her friend was a sight in breeches and a cream blouse. She stood slowly; eyes wary.

"It's good to see you, Merielle," Esta said, closing the gap and dropping a kiss on her cheek. She swallowed sudden nerves. "Tell me what's come to pass with Reid?"

Merielle let out a long sigh. "I do not know whether to hug you or strangle you," she said, her hands clenched at her sides. "Leaving the way you did…leaving me to deal with your impulsiveness…" She took a long gasping breath, tears in her vibrant green eyes. Esta's heart broke at the sight of her friend in such distress.

"I'm sorry for causing you trouble." She clamped her teeth on her bottom lip, her own tears close to spilling. Was this another loss she'd have to bear?

Merielle studied her for another long moment then pulled Esta into her arms. "Oh, my friend," she said. "Are you well? The stories I have heard!"

Esta relaxed into the hug and a sense of calm slid over her. This was a friendship she couldn't afford to lose; her first close female friend and she had almost lost her over a man. "I'm well and so is my sister."

"I am glad." She drew back and studied Esta, her brows drawn down. "I do not know what has passed on the ocean, my friend, but I must tell you that everything has changed here. Reid is furious and will not take you back… if that is what you want." She took a deep breath as if battling her anger again. "He has paid off all the workers and said he will not ask for the money back for the work on your estate. I think that is very generous."

"Yes, it is." Until that moment, Esta hadn't thought of the debt she might owe her betrothed. Another debt! Well, she wouldn't rest until Reid had his money back. She reached for Merielle's hand. "I never intended to hurt you or Reid."

Merielle gave a delicate snort. "I will recover, but Reid will not, I fear. I do not understand how you could have thrown his heart away like that!"

Esta drew herself up. "When I knew Nikolas planned to find Sam I couldn't sit here and wait for the outcome."

"And what did you think you could do?"

"Be the voice of reason? I don't know. Anything was preferable to sitting here when Sam's entire future was at stake."

Merielle gasped. "You've fallen in love with him. A pirate! Is that wise?"

"Yes, I love him. What choice do I have but to support him? I thought you'd understand."

"I understand love," Merielle said, "but Nikolas is, well, magnificent."

"Careful, Merielle. I value your friendship. I wouldn't want you to say anything I couldn't forgive."

"But how can it ever work? Samael is in prison and will stay there if the king has anything to say about it."

Esta wrapped her arms around herself to stem the panic when she thought of Sam in a damp, dark cell. "Nikolas will get him out. He has to." She hated the pity in Merielle's eyes.

"Yes, of course," Merielle said. "Nikolas will help if he can."

* * *

Sam sat in the dank cell humming a tune his mother had used to settle him as a child. The gentle words of the song pulled him back from the brink of panic - his heart slowed and finally he could relax against the stone wall. The stench of the slop pail hit him anew as he took a long deep breath. Two days confinement and still his mind and body refused to accept what he had become - a captive. He tried not to think about everything he'd lost in the last few months but, deprived of light, cold and hungry, it was impossible to be optimistic.

He kept running through the choices he'd made and doubting them. He'd been happy roaming the high seas, living off other people's success, not thinking too much of anything deeper.

But the niggling feeling of being an outsider had long been there. It had been there because he was an interloper in his own family. But that was better than this - stuck in the dark and fighting panic! He liked to think he was as sane as the next man but the last two days in prison had taught him how tenuous his grip on sanity really was.

He could trace his slump back to the moment he decided to find his mother. He'd been on a downhill slide ever since. And now here he was, deprived of freedom and dependent on others for everything. He may as well be dead. The anger that boiled in his gut kept him from believing death would be preferable. *That's it Delacost, stay angry. It's the only thing that will keep you sane!*

So deep was he in his doldrums that he didn't hear the approach of the guard until the man appeared at the cell bars with a lantern.

"Visitor for you, Delacost."

He squinted at the dark figure beside the guard and sniffed a faint perfume on the air.

Esta! He stood slowly, muscles screaming at being asked to move, and limped over to the gate. Her perfume reminded him there was sunshine and fresh air somewhere out there. And love.

"Five minutes." The guard lit a brand that was shoved into a holder near the cell and stomped back up the hallway.

She threw herself against the bars. "Are you well?"

He laughed - the sound halfway to insanity. He stepped closer until he could lay his forehead on hers. "I will prevail." It was the best he could do but not as reassuring as he'd hoped.

"I had to see you, dearest. I was losing my mind not knowing." He heard her swallow. "It's horrible here." Then a sniff as she forced back tears. "Has Nikolas been to see you?"

"You're my sole visitor apart from when the guards deliver food and water. "

"What's he doing? I must see him, beg him to do something."

"Hush, my love." His heart pounded at the panic in her voice. He couldn't be strong if she fell to pieces. "Can you tell me anything? When's the trial?"

She gave a sharp intake of breath. "The day after tomorrow. At dawn. You didn't know?"

The hair on the nape of his neck lifted sending a shiver over his scalp. He was literally being kept in the dark.

"I'm sure Nikolas is scrambling around trying his best to get me off the hook. If you see him, please ask if he can visit me?" Damn it, that was too much like begging. He had never stooped so low.

"I'll do everything I can, Sam, and I'll work on my own plan if all else fails."

He broke out in a cold sweat at her words. "What plan?"

"It's better that you don't know, my love, and I'll only use it if I'm desperate."

"Tell me, Esta."

"Hush." She drew him toward her, small fists bunched in his shirt. Her lips met his between the bars and he savored her sweet fragrance, sank into her lush warmth until his troubles started to fade. He groaned when she moved back.

She took a deep breath. "Have courage. I'll not fail you." With one last kiss, she was gone, striding away until she was lost in the gloom of the passageway.

* * *

As Esta hurried away from Sam she battled for composure. She'd never seen him so undone and it terrified her. *Pull yourself together woman!* No sense giving into the desperate fear that ate at her. Fear would lead to weakness and she couldn't afford to be weak when she might be his only hope. She must be the spider, devious and hidden, hatching her plan for the day when it might be required. Cold reason must be her strength but oh, how she had needed the time spent with him, the kisses shared!

The conditions he was kept in brought tears to her eyes that she brushed away angrily. That cell was suitable for the lowest of the low and her love was certainly not that. Not in her eyes and hopefully not in the eyes of his brother. Surely Nikolas had a plan that would save his last remaining brother? He could not turn his back just to save his pride and position. Could he?

She didn't know the admiral well enough and, while he had shown some signs of wanting a connection with Sam, his brotherly love hadn't been overwhelming.

As she passed the last of the cells before the stairs, a hissing drew her attention. She looked to the left and five sets of glowing eyes made her pause. Elven eyes!

"I hope you have said your goodbyes, Lady Moonlight." That voice belonged to Sam's second in command, Nande. "He will pay for his alliance with the *Lenweri* just as we will pay for his betrayal of us."

Esta clenched her jaws so tightly she heard something crack. "You chose your fate when you attacked the admiral. Captain Delacost had a plan that would have saved you all or at least given you a chance."

Nande snorted. "No plan would have sufficed save the one I counseled. We should have found a vantage from which we could have been victors over the kingdom sailors. Instead he chose to negotiate. I knew we were doomed unless we fought. Better to die fighting than go meekly to the gallows."

She shook her head. She had liked the *Lenweri* leader in a different time. "I'm sorry this has come to pass. I see no hope for you and your men."

He lifted his head as his companions hissed again. "I need no pity from you, Lady. Look to your own troubles and your past and be afraid."

She backed away from the cell and hurried up the stairs, hissing and cat calls chasing her. She met the guard coming down.

"Wait at the top of the stairs, lass. I'll quiet this lot and be back to unlock the door."

As she waited, Esta couldn't settle the trembling that beset her entire body. The elves hated her. They would expose her for the lying, stealing woman she was. When that happened, she and her family would lose everything. She couldn't let that happen, but how would she prevent it?

Katrine awaited her outside the prison. She took one look and drew Esta into her arms. "Tell me," she whispered, steering her older sister toward the coach they had hired. They entered the carriage and she told Katrine all she had experienced.

"It's far worse than I imagined for Sam," Esta said. "And what of myself? I can't undo the things I've done in the past and neither can you."

Katrine chewed her lip. "We could run - to Brightcastle. Hetty would take us in."

She shook her head. "You run if you like. I have to be here for Sam."

Katrine's eyes blazed. "He wouldn't want you to suffer! And you don't have the protection of being the sibling of the admiral. What if Nikolas makes you the scapegoat?"

Esta shook her head. "Merielle wouldn't let him do that."

Katrine chewed her fingernail. "It's the *Lenweri's* word against ours. Our crew will be loyal. I'll travel back to the estate and make sure there's nothing to link us with smuggling. We have no ship and the estate is as poor as a church mouse. We'll deny it. As long as there's no proof."

A small chink of hope pried its way into Esta's heart. "Do you think so?"

She nodded. "I'll make it so. You worry about your pirate and I'll cover our backs."

She launched herself off the seat and embraced Katrine. "You always know what to do in a crisis, Kat. I love you so much."

"Don't think this means I approve of you and that man," she said. "I'm doing this for you and for our family."

Esta nodded. "I know that. I intend to show you Samael Delacost is worthy of my love."

"I hope for your sake he is, and you get to show me how worthy. There's much water to flow under that bridge, Sister."

Esta nodded again and settled back beside Katrine for the trip back to the castle. She closed her eyes and prayed the Goddess would deliver salvation for Sam - prayed that she wouldn't have to enact her plan.

CHAPTER 22

SAM was led into the chamber in chains. The day suited his mood. Charcoal gray clouds rolled in across the sea bringing with them driving rain and howling winds. Even here in the king's audience chamber, the crash of the waves on the rocks below was an ever-present reminder of nature's fury. The wind forced its way into every small crack and the room was bitterly cold. Sam was even colder, soaked to the skin after his trip from the prison. But it was no worse than many occasions at sea.

By the look of the crowd gathered, all the nobility and guild masters were in attendance. He cast his eye around for Esta but didn't see her. Despite the cold, he broke out in a sweat.

The possibility that she wouldn't attend his hearing hadn't occurred to him. In all this madness that was his new reality, she was a beacon of hope and light.

But of course, she wouldn't be here. She had a life and a reputation to uphold. Being associated with him wouldn't help her one bit. She said she had a plan which would certainly involve her throwing herself on Nikolas's mercy or that of the king or queen. Much good that would do. Still he longed for a glimpse of her beautiful face, the sound of her honeyed voice.

King Beniel and Nikolas stood together on the dais, overlooking him as his chains were tethered to a ring in the stone floor. He closed his eyes and sought that inner place of calm he usually possessed. Today it deserted him as it had since his imprisonment. Inside, all was a-churn, like the restless ocean below. He fought harder, imagining the sea as a mill pond, blue and calm, but the gray and the cold and the restless energy wouldn't be banished. He swallowed hard and opened his eyes.

King Beniel's icy gaze greeted him. Cold, blue and as hard as granite - no mercy. Nande and the other *Lenweri* would receive no clemency from the monarch, especially with the recent battles the kingdom had faced against the dark elves. But he was Samael Delacost and his father had taught him never to give in; never to show fear. He looked the king in the eye and bowed as well as he could in chains. The monarch was unmoved, but Nikolas frowned. *Damn him!*

The prosecutor stepped forward. He was a tall, thin man in black robes with an oiled black moustache and goatee beard.

"Samael Delacost," he said, "you stand accused of piracy and murder, of failing to uphold the King's Law and of associating with the enemy." The man turned to the king. "I think you'll agree, Your Majesty, that these are the most serious of crimes."

"Indeed, Counselor, I do. I intend to see justice for the kingdom of Thorius in this matter."

Sam tried to keep any feelings from his face, tried to find that tranquil core as the prosecutor spoke again.

"I intend to prove this man before you did, in fact, commit all the crimes listed and incited others to aid him. He was the captain of the ship from whence these *Lenweri* scum we house originated."

His crew were still in the cells then?

"Call your witnesses, Counselor," the king said.

"Your Majesty, Admiral Cosara and members of the court. It has long been the case that a scoundrel named the Singing Pirate roamed the oceans from south of Shawmere and far into the north. The deeds were done at night with the help of the night vision of a *Lenweri* crew. I believe this man before you, Samael Delacost, is the Singing Pirate. I call Lord Cosara to the stand."

Nikolas stepped forward, not looking at Sam.

"Lord Cosara, you are admiral of the King's Fleet and as such, your word is beyond question. Was this man, Samael Delacost, found in the company of *Lenweri*?"

Now Nikolas looked at him, just a glance as if to check who the prosecutor was naming. "Yes, Counselor, this is the man I found consorting with the elves."

"Did it appear they had been aboard his ship?"

"I believe that to be the case," Nikolas said.

Sam cleared his throat. "The admiral never saw *Lenweri* aboard my ship when under my captaincy."

The prosecutor glared at him. "You will have a chance to defend yourself when I've finished, Delacost." He addressed Nikolas. "Admiral, tell those assembled of the events that led up to you taking ship in search of the scoundrel, the Singing Pirate."

"I knew of the Singing Pirate rumored to lead a *Lenweri* crew in night raids on merchant ships in the area. I had also heard the name Samael Delacost and now know they are one and the same person. The night raids recently escalated, more of them and increasingly bold. They also became more deadly. Sailors were being killed and wounded and trade was being affected. The matter was sufficiently serious for me to mount a mission to find and detain the person or persons responsible for the crimes. I believed, because of the night raids and reports from affected ship's captains, that the perpetrator of most of these crimes was the Singing Pirate."

"So, you tracked him down?" the prosecutor asked.

Nikolas nodded. "It wasn't easy. I finally found his ship, *Silver Lady*, at anchor in a bay on one of the central reef islands. It's an ideal refuge and very difficult to enter and leave."

"But you found it and there you found this man, Delacost?"

"I did. His crew, the *Lenweri*—,"

"I object, Your Majesty," Sam said. "The admiral assumed they were my crew."

"Perhaps you had better avoid assumptions, Counselor," the king said.

"Very well. Admiral, you found this man in the company of *Lenweri*, did you not?"

Nikolas inclined his head. "I did."

"And what was the attitude of this man when you confronted him?"

"He tried to negotiate his way out of the situation," Nikolas said, "but the *Lenweri* with him attacked us."

"Could you describe what happened then, Admiral?"

Nikolas proceeded to detail the ensuing battle and aftermath. Sam had to admit it was a fair summary and included his own decision to fight against the *Lenweri*.

The prosecutor appeared incredulous. "This man aided you in the battle?"

"We fought side by side," Nikolas said. "I have no doubt the situation could have been much worse without his aid."

"Come now, Admiral, without the actions of this rogue, you wouldn't have been in that position."

Nikolas nodded and Sam ground his teeth.

"Admiral," the prosecutor continued, "why do you think Delacost aided you?"

"There were ladies present and I believe the accused was trying to protect them."

"Ladies?" the counselor said. "How were there ladies present?"

Nikolas squared his shoulders. "I was using their services to find the pirate."

"What help could women possibly be in this respect?"

"I'd prefer not to say."

"This is most unusual, Admiral. Who were these women?"

Nikolas remained silent.

Sam listened fascinated at the details that had been covered up. What did it mean?

"Does it matter?" Sam asked. "We are judging my actions here, not those of the ladies."

The counselor looked down his nose. "Anything might be relevant. At the very least, these women are witnesses and I must insist they be named."

The king cleared his throat. "They will be called if necessary. At this time, I don't believe they have anything to add that the admiral can't provide."

The prosecutor frowned and turned back to Nikolas. "Admiral, have you or any of your men witnessed Delacost in the act of piracy?"

"I have not, but I have one of my captains in this room who says he can identify the captain of the pirate ship, *Silver Lady*."

"Very well, Admiral, you may step down and I will call the next witness."

Days of darkness, poor food and no exercise were taking their toll. Sam would have given anything for a chair. He shifted his weight and glanced around the hall again.

There she is!

She stood at the side of the hall half hidden by a pillar. Their eyes met and a shiver ran through him. She was here as promised.

And then he checked himself. How did he sink this low that he relied upon others to save him? That was the slippery slope to ruin and he was on it and halfway down if he was any judge.

Soft! That was him! A landlocked ocean man who should never have placed himself in this position. He had allowed his yearning for family and the lure of a woman to lead him astray. But unwanted, his gaze returned to the lady beside the pillar and the anger oozed away. She was everything he wanted. If he had to give up his freedom to have her, so be it.

Who am I jesting? I'll never have her. Never have anything but a prison cell or a noose. And better a noose than a dungeon where his spirit would die long before his body. The momentary fire drained into the cold hall and he closed his eyes.

A chair! I'd kill for a chair.

"Captain Derota," the prosecutor said, "is the man you see before you the very man who boarded your ship at night, stole your cargo and killed your men?"

He opened his eyes to the accusing gaze of the last captain he had stolen from. He must stay focused if he was to have any hope of defending himself.

"It is. He and his *Lenweri* boarded my ship at night and I lost a number of my crew."

"Don't worry, Captain," the prosecutor said. "The crown will see justice done."

Sam roused himself. "Stick to the facts," he growled.

"Do you deny you stole from this man and killed his sailors, Delacost?"

He swallowed hard. This was it, the moment he had dreaded. "I deny killing his men. I killed no one on that ship."

"Ha! So you admit you boarded," the prosecutor said. "You were the captain, Delacost! What your crew did was under your orders. You knew when you set foot on that ship there was a chance of bloodshed. You are responsible!"

Sam shook his head. "I authorized minimal force. I want goods not lives."

The prosecutor sneered. "You're a highly trained swordsman, one of the best. What chance do these men have against you?"

"As I said, I authorized minimal force." He took a deep breath to stem his racing heart. "And when I entered the fight, I dealt non-lethal blows."

"Oh, I'm sure you did, Delacost," the lawyer said. "Pirates are known for their restraint and compassion."

Sam squared his shoulders. "It's his word against mine that I hurt anyone."

"You admit to boarding his ship! You admit to taking his goods! That's enough to convict you of piracy. The penalty, Your Majesty, for piracy with loss of life…is death. That's what I'll be asking for. Death by hanging for Samael Delacost."

A cheer went up from the court, loud enough to drown out the pounding surf below. He glanced around the chamber and saw hostile faces on all sides. They wanted his head. As if they hadn't all robbed in their own way. The nobility was well known for taking more than their share in taxes from the people who depended on them.

He was guilty, no doubt about that. All that would save him now was Nikolas standing up and declaring his relationship to the accused. Would he do that?

The admiral's face was carved in stone. A muscle twitched along his jaw and he stared straight ahead. A war went on inside, that was clear. Or he hoped it did.

The king stood. "I think we have heard enough. I will give my ruling." He turned to Sam. "Samael Delacost. You stand accused of piracy and murder, of associating with *Lenweri*, the enemy of this kingdom. The evidence is clear to me. What do you plead?"

"I plead not guilty to all but the piracy, Your Majesty." He stood proud as the hall again erupted in anger. He looked for Esta, who stood exposed, brown eyes wide, her head shaking from side to side. Her lips moved as though she argued with herself.

"State your case, Delacost," the king said.

"Your Majesty, I admit I was a pirate, that I had a *Lenweri* crew. They never gave me any reason to think they were enemies of the kingdom. I know their people have caused us concern, but I don't believe they were of the *Sis Lenweri* faction."

"You had to know it would be looked upon unfavorably," the counselor said.

"I used the *Lenweri* for their night vision. We could board ships under the cover of darkness and be away before anyone knew. That was our plan. I wanted to hurt no one physically."

"Still, you did," King Beniel said.

Sam nodded. "Men were injured and killed and for that I'm sorry." He considered his next words. "When the admiral came looking for me, I stood with him when my crew turned on me. I protected the women. The admiral and I fought back to back. I almost lost my own life. That has to mean something."

The king inclined his head. "We are grateful that the admiral has come back to us and that the ladies are safe. However, I must state that without you, there would have been no need for the mission at all. The murder of kingdom citizens led to the admiral taking steps to find and stop you. I must make an example of you and see justice done for the men who never came back."

Sam looked at Nikolas, who finally met his gaze. Now was the time for him to declare his brother, if he had the courage to do so. Nikolas frowned and time stood still as the wind howled around the castle.

The king seemed oblivious to Nikolas as he cleared his throat. No doubt this was merely another distasteful decision his Majesty had to make in a long line of them for this day. But it was Sam's life on the line. *Nikolas do something!*

"Samael Delacost. I find you guilty of piracy and of consorting with the enemy. As such you have committed treason against the crown. Of the murder charge, I must grant you the benefit of the doubt in this case. There is no proof you killed anyone, and you behaved commendably when called to make a decision for or against the admiral." The king paused, a smile on his lips. Sam stifled a growl. Treason and piracy were still enough to get him hanged and the monarch had the gall to look pleased!

"Samael Delacost," King Beniel continued, "you have been found guilty of piracy and treason. I sentence you to death by hanging. No appeal will be allowed, and the sentence will pass tomorrow."

He went ice cold deep in his bowels. His heart gave a giant leap then slowed as though it was winding down. He took a slow breath, and everything came back into focus. There were gasps from the crowd and he turned to find Esta. She stepped from her place against the wall and walked toward the dais. She looked at Nikolas, her teeth gritted and muttering as she passed. She mounted the stairs and was restrained by the guards.

"Let me pass," she said, trying to shake off their hands.

What was she trying to do? He was suddenly terrified as she fought to get to Nikolas.

"What is the meaning of this intrusion, Lady Aranati?" the king asked. "I will be hearing no more petitions for today. Kindly retire and see me on the morrow."

The king turned away and Esta broke free, lunging for Nikolas and clawing her way up his tunic until she could whisper close to his ear. His eyes widened at whatever she said, and he turned King Beniel. "Excuse me, Your Majesty, may I impose on you for a few moments? I need a private word."

The king frowned but nodded and the two men moved away into the back of the hall. Sam couldn't hear a word that was said but King Beniel looked at Esta and then Sam. There were more muffled discussions after which Beniel and Nikolas returned to the throne area.

"If it pleases the court," the king said. "I have reason to grant a stay of execution for a period of two days while I ponder recent information that has come to light."

The crowd buzzed with the news, an angry hive if ever he had heard one.

"Tell me what's going on, dammit!" he said. "Lady, what did you tell the admiral? Lady Aranati!"

But she turned and hurried away, two guards close on her heels as if she were a common criminal. She didn't even look in his direction.

He was tugged around, and his gaze fell upon Nikolas who stared at him openmouthed.

What did she say? Damn her, he had to know. "Cosara, what's going on?"

The guard at his side swore. "You've been given an extra two days you don't deserve, Delacost. Isn't that enough for you?"

He was hauled from the room, jeers and curses following. Any moment he expected to feel the sharp stab of steel, but he passed safely through the doors and corridors outside. In minutes he was back in his cell, in the gloom with only rats and roaches for company.

"Send me the admiral," Sam said to his jailor. "I have to know what she said."

The man frowned. "I don't know what you're talking about lad, but I'll see what I can do. No guarantees." The man turned and tramped back up the passage, leaving him in darkness.

CHAPTER 23

WHAT have I done? Esta's body shook and her chamber walls spun. *And will it be enough?* That she still had the presence of mind to wonder amazed her. The whispered declaration she had made to Nikolas could change everything for both her and Sam. It could ruin her, and it might be too little to save him. The king had granted two days. *Two days!*

She had to see Nikolas, convince him to come out in the open about his brother. She had given him a stay of two days; Nikolas could reverse the order altogether. Damn him! Why was he so proud?

She jumped at an abrupt knock on the door. Her maid scurried over and opened it.

Nikolas swept through, his turquoise eyes stormy. "What the devil are you playing at, Madam?"

She stood and looked him in the eye. "This is no game. A man's life is at stake and you're doing nothing."

"I'm doing all I can. I've spoken with the king daily; presented Delacost's behavior in the best light I can. It has made no difference."

"You know of what I speak," she said, conscious of the maid in the next room.

Nikolas's eyes darted toward the bedchamber.

Oh yes, he should be afraid of exposure. He must be furious to come here and confront me.

"I'm vulnerable, Lady Aranati," he said. "There are things in my past I still haven't overcome. This revelation might be the end of me."

She shook her head. "So you place yourself over him?"

"Damn right I do. I have a wife to think of and other family."

"Oh yes, you certainly do have other family, Admiral. It's a pity you can't bring yourself to care enough about *them*."

"You're being unfair," he said. "Anyway, I came here to discuss what you told me. Is it true?"

"I'm not in the habit of lying," she said. He didn't know what she was capable of, thank the Goddess. "I don't think it will be enough, but you had better hope it is for the sake of your precious reputation."

"I'll send the royal midwife to have a look at you," Nikolas said.

"Don't you dare," she said. "I'll be perfectly fine."

A muscle in his jaw tensed and she feared he would force her to undergo an examination. "I think it best you return to your estate."

"I will go nowhere until I know his fate." She folded her arms under her breasts and waited.

"Very well." He nodded and left the room, muttering under his breath.

She sighed and sat back on the chair in front of the fire. She must see Sam and explain to him what she had done.

Esta stood in the alcove of the prison entrance and took deep breaths to slow her heart. Katrine, against her better judgment she said, had cast a spell on her. The enchantment would make her invisible for a short period of time, perhaps less than an hour. None of this would be necessary if King Beniel had granted her visiting rights.

Voices came from the command room, raised voices. What were they doing? It sounded like gambling. Just her luck that tonight of all nights there were more men than usual on duty.

Refusing to be cowed by the challenge, she said a prayer to the Goddess and opened the heavy oak door just enough for her to slip inside. It moved silently. She inched along the entry hall until she could see the men. They were dicing and drinking and with luck would never hear her.

Staying as close to the wall as she could, Esta slipped through the command room, not taking a breath until she was in the corridor on the other side. As she moved down the hall and past the compartments, she dared not look into the cells for fear of what she'd see. She heard plenty though – groans and soft squishes and water tinkling. She didn't like to imagine what was behind those noises. Heart thumping, and worried about how much time had passed, she began her descent into the dungeon. It was so dark she could barely make out the steps and had to place her foot over the edge and feel for each level.

Step by agonizing step, she traveled the stairs and crept past the *Lenweri*. She knew they were there because they spoke in their tongue. Their conversation stopped as she neared their cell and didn't resume until she was past. They knew something was amiss! But no alarm was raised.

Now which one was Sam's cell? She couldn't remember. Was it four or five cells past the elves? Damn her memory! There was nothing for it. At the fourth cell she whispered his name, but no one answered. It was the same for the fifth cell.

Panic hit as she worried he'd been shifted. Were they keeping him in a secret place? She moved to the sixth cell. "Sam!"

A shadow moved in the dark. "What the devil do you want?"

Relief washed over her and her knees went weak. "Sam! It's me. I came to explain."

"It's time someone did," he said, looking over her left shoulder. "Why can't I see you?"

"Katrine has done this so I may visit with you in secret. The king denied permission."

"Never mind, what the hell did you tell Nikolas that gave me the stay of execution?"

"He hasn't been to see you yet?"

"No one has been to see me." He sounded angry, alone and despairing.

"I don't have much time. Come to the bars so I can touch you."

"Just tell me what you said, damn it."

She sighed. He wasn't going to make this easy. "I'm here to explain, but I need to touch you."

At first there was silence but then a rustling told her he had stood. His large hand covered hers on the bars and she saw his faint outline. "I've missed you."

He still loved her, still wanted her. All she had to do was make this work. "I've missed you too. I was terrified I wouldn't be allowed to tell you that."

"You weren't. What game are they playing at?"

She shook her head. "You're being kept isolated. Nikolas is worried for his reputation."

"Some brother!"

"He has trauma in his past that still haunts him," she said. How to tell him her plan?

"Tell me what you told Nikolas."

She took a deep breath and slowly let it out. "I told him I was expecting your child."

"What!"

"Hush, they'll hear and come down. I had to do something and that was all I could think of."

"This will ruin you if it gets out."

"It had the desired effect. I have two days to get Nikolas to reveal you're his brother. I'll petition him again this evening."

He slid his arms through the bars and around her, pulling her against him. His lips found her forehead and she tilted her head up so they could kiss. Despite his desperation, Sam's mouth was tender on hers, exploring her lips, and venturing inside to capture her tongue. She so needed his body wrapped around hers, but reality crushed her desire. This might be the last time she touched him in this life.

"I love you, Samael Delacost. Don't you ever forget."

"That sounds final."

"I don't mean it to," she said. "It's just that we've had so little time together, you might believe you're not important."

There was a long pause during which Esta's nerves stretched taut. *What if he doesn't want me?*

"How did you know exactly what I needed to hear? That I matter to you?"

"You matter more than anything else in my life." She fumbled under her cloak for the knife and pulled it out. "That's why I want you to have this." She passed the weapon through the bars and was rewarded by his gasp.

"I can't take this."

Anger flared. "What do you mean? If all else fails —"

"If all else fails, we'll have tried everything."

"Not everything! I can't let you give up. If your sentence isn't changed, you must fight your way free. Or I'll break you out with Katrine's help."

The knife dropped to the stone floor. His hands found hers. "I must take a stand for what's right. I've lived the life of an outlaw and people have suffered. If the Goddess sees fit to condemn me then so be it. In the end, I'll have honor."

"Honor! And how will that sustain me when you're gone or in prison?"

He let out a long breath. "I know you love me, but I want you to respect me as well. I want that for myself too. What life would we have if I escaped with that sentence hanging over my head? I'd rather die than be hunted."

"But, Sam—"

"No!" His voice was sharp, determined. "No more, Esta. I've drawn a line in the sand, and I won't step over it again. Not for you or anyone. I've had a lot of time to think in here. A lot of time to ponder all the hurt I've caused; to reflect on the men who won't come home to their loved ones because of me."

"It wasn't entirely your fault."

"If not mine, whose? I raised that crew. I decided on its purpose. At the time, I thought it was the only life I could choose. Now I know better. I won't go back."

"Then there is naught for me to do but speak to your brother."

"There's one more thing you can do."

"Anything!"

"If the worst happens and I hang for this, find my mother and father and tell them what happened to me. I couldn't stand it if they never knew why I didn't come back."

Esta couldn't help the sob that escaped. "I will." She clutched him through the bars. "Goodbye, my love," he said, and his lips found hers.

She pulled away, leaving him in the dark and leaving her heart with him forever.

CHAPTER 24

ESTA hadn't slept for two days and now the time had come for the king to make his final decision. She had made two more pleas to Nikolas to declare his brother. They had fallen on deaf ears. Nikolas was a good man, but he had let Sam down. She tried to be impartial, endeavored to see both sides of the issue but the truth was, blood was blood. Nikolas owed his brother and she would not allow him to shirk his duty.

She took her place in the hall, in disguise, as she was told not to attend today. Nothing would keep her away from Sam in his hour of need. She couldn't use the invisibility spell today as she needed to be able to be seen if the worst should happen.

Sam was led into the hall in chains and tethered to the ring before the throne. She trembled at the sight of him. He had lost more weight and was in desperate need of a wash. Her free-spirited man was not coping well in the dungeons and nobody seemed concerned about his health.

Damn them all!

She watched him scan the hall and knew he searched for her. He'd never recognize her in the black wig and workaday clothes. Esta had donned the garb of a farmwife, as many petitioned the king on occasions like this. His eye swept over her with nary a pause. Her heart ached when she realized he'd think she hadn't come to his sentencing.

But there was little she could do about that. Straightening her shoulders, she breathed her nerves away and kept hold of an image of him as she had first seen him - handsome and defiant and free. He would be that way again.

The prosecutor cleared his throat. "The next matter before His Majesty is the sentencing of Samael Delacost, pirate, murderer and traitor."

"Counselor," King Beniel said. "This man was not convicted of murder."

The prosecutor's face turned bright red. "Sorry, Your Majesty, please forget I mentioned it." He turned back to the people. "You'll recall there was a two day stay of sentencing owing to new information presented at the recent trial. King Beniel has considered the matters brought before him and is ready to announce the sentence. Delacost, prepare yourself."

Esta couldn't breathe. Nikolas stood on the dais as though he'd been turned to stone. She searched for some indication of his intent but found none.

The king stood. "Samael Delacost, you have been declared guilty of piracy and treason. I have deliberated on the news I received two days ago and have found it insufficient to reverse the death sentence."

She froze, unable to think, to take in the enormity of the news. She had hoped it wouldn't come to. Now she had sullied her reputation for naught.

No! It had given her precious time with Sam that no one could take away, not even the king.

He continued. "This leaves me with only one duty and that is to authorize your execution, which will take place this afternoon."

Esta sagged against the wall, desperate to decide what she should do. Nikolas looked more on edge than ever. *Do something!*

Soldiers surrounded Sam and untethered him from the ring in the floor. Soon he'd be beyond help. She started toward the front of the hall, quietly, while blood pounded in her head. She was steps away from the group around Sam when Nikolas caught her eye. He seemed to recognize her, for he frowned. She sent him a silent plea and he shook his head.

Very well, Admiral, she thought, I've given you every chance to reveal your secret.

"Your Majesty," she said, but nobody seemed to hear. She tried once more. "Your Majesty!" People nearby turned to her but not those who mattered. Nikolas strode toward her.

"You'll ruin everything," he said.

"What? Your precious naval career? Your standing in this shallow court? Merielle must be so proud of you!"

Nikolas clutched her arm, tight enough for her to feel his strength. "I have a plan."

She hesitated for just one second before making her decision. She screamed at the top of her lungs and collapsed at the admiral's feet. The hall went deathly silent and Nikolas crouched beside her, patting her face and muttering under his breath.

"Don't you dare expose me, Lady. I have a plan."

Esta pretended to be unconscious until she spied the royal slippers from under her lashes. She moaned and tried to sit up. When her eyes opened, the king's face loomed before her.

"Are you well, Madam?"

"I must speak with you, Your Majesty. There is something you must know about the admiral and Samael Delacost."

Nikolas hissed. "Your Highness, Lady Aranati is making mischief."

The King helped her up, his face red. "Has this court not been disgraced enough of late? Must we have women in disguise screaming and collapsing? Not to mention your scene of the other day. Madam, explain yourself."

"Your Majesty," Nikolas said, "let me take care of this matter."

The king turned to Nikolas. "I wish to hear what she has to say, Admiral, and I will. Speak Lady Aranati."

She couldn't look at Nikolas for fear his very expression would freeze the words on her tongue. *This must be said.* "Lord Cosara and Samael Delacost are brothers, Your Majesty."

The king lurched backward, his eyes wide. He turned to first Nikolas and then Sam, his eyes narrowed. "Can this be true? Lord Cosara?"

Nikolas looked down at his feet as the seconds ticked by. Finally, his gaze rose to the king's. "It's true, Your Majesty. We share a mother."

"And you were going to keep this secret? You would allow your brother to go to the gallows?"

"I would never have allowed that to happen, Your Majesty."

Esta snorted.

"As the brother of a Thorian lord," King Beniel said, "Delacost has certain privileges. One of those is to choose life in prison over the noose." He turned to his soldiers. "Clear the court. I wish to speak to the admiral in private. Leave this woman and the prisoner here as well."

King Beniel was silent as the hall cleared. When they were alone, Esta joined Sam.

"You came," he said. "What did you do this time?"

"I told the king about Nikolas," she said. "I couldn't let him deny you. He said he had a plan, but I couldn't wait any longer."

He nodded. "That's why the room was cleared. Good disguise, Esta, I hardly recognize you even now."

"What do you think will happen?"

He shrugged. "The choice is mine, it seems."

Her head spun and she clutched his arm for support. A small sob escaped despite her attempts to suppress it. "You're saved!"

"And the credit is all yours, Lady. However, I won't spend the rest of my life in prison."

Fear replaced elation as she wondered what he meant by the remark. "Don't do anything silly, I beg of you. I've already told you I can't live without you. We'll find a way to exist."

"Are you listening to yourself? As if I could merely exist when I've lived with the waves across my bow and a fresh wind in my hair. I won't swap that for a prison cell."

"Have I risked everything in vain?" she asked, her fingers digging into his forearm.

Someone cleared their throat behind her, and she turned to the stormy gaze of the admiral. "What have you done, Lady? I told you I had a plan."

"I did what you refused to. Sam deserves to be acknowledged and now he is."

Nikolas looked him in the eye. "I wouldn't have let you hang, please believe that. I had a plan that would have saved you and left my family unblemished. Now I fear the king will replace me as he replaced Kain Jazara. King Beniel doesn't like scandal."

The king joined them, but she barely noticed. Had she treated Nikolas unfairly? She didn't wish to believe her actions might ruin him, but she also couldn't have risked Sam.

"You're correct, Admiral," Beniel said. "We do not like scandal. When the queen hears of this, she will haul you over the coals."

Nikolas squared his shoulders. "I'll face what must be faced now that Lady Aranati has exposed my relationship to Delacost."

Esta winced at his tone.

"We have to decide on a plan now that this information has come to light," the king said. "What to do with this pirate who seems to have some good at his center and a valid blood connection to one of my biggest supporters? Also, do we make this relationship public?"

Nikolas's jaw tensed. He wouldn't wish to be publicly linked to Sam but if her pirate was safe, she didn't care.

"I'd suggest caution, Your Majesty," Nikolas said. "Let us keep this between us for now."

"There is still the matter of what to do," the king said. "Delacost will not hang but a prison sentence must be served."

"Your Majesty," Sam said, "might I suggest hard labor? Lock me away in that cell and you may as well hang me now."

Esta held her breath as the monarch considered.

"I will take counsel from my wife. She will know what to do in this instance," the king said. "Until I make my decision, the admiral must take responsibility for Delacost. Do you agree to this Lord Cosara?"

Nikolas drew a long breath and slowly exhaled. He glared at Sam and then turned to the king. "Your Majesty, I'm sorry this has threatened to bring scandal down on your throne. I did everything I could to prevent that. It's generous of you to allow Delacost prison release under my care and I'll see to it he doesn't escape your justice."

"Now wait a minute —" Sam said, but Esta dug her fingers into his arm again.

"Did you have something to add, Delacost?" the king asked.

Sam frowned at Esta who shook her head.

"No, Your Majesty," Sam said. "You've been very fair."

"What will the arrangements be, Admiral?" King Beniel fixed Nikolas with his sharp blue gaze, his slippered foot tapping the stone floor.

Nikolas straightened and looked the king in the eye. "Delacost can come back to my estate until you make your pronouncement. I'll stay there to ensure nothing happens. If you could send a rider as soon as you've reached a decision, I'd appreciate it, Your Majesty."

The king nodded. "Very well. Retire to your estate and I'll do as you request. Delacost, this is possibly more than you deserve. I might still throw you in a cell. See that you do not do anything to make me regret releasing you."

Sam bowed as well as he could in irons. "Thank you, Your Majesty."

The king swept from the hall and when Esta turned to Nikolas, he was shaking his head. "I hold you completely responsible, Lady Aranati. If I live to regret this, let me assure you, I have a long memory."

Her face went hot. She had made herself a powerful enemy, but it was for Sam and she couldn't regret it. "So be it, Admiral."

Nikolas led Sam from the room via the back door and she followed, wondering what the next few days would bring.

CHAPTER 25

ESTA sat by the crackling fire in her sitting room on the Cosara estate. She tried to concentrate on her embroidery. Sharpening a knife would have been more appropriate with her nerves so on edge. After being smuggled out of the castle, she had endured an uncomfortable carriage ride to the admiral's estate and retired to her room exhausted.

A fitful night's sleep had done naught to make her feel better and then today Sam had virtually ignored her. He had spent the day mucking out the stables and when he was inside the house, he took care to speak to her as little as possible.

She didn't know what to believe. He must be angry with her though she could not puzzle out why. Or perhaps he had realized he didn't love her after all? She didn't wish to contemplate a life without him, but it seemed she must. After all she had given up, she wondered if there was anything left worth salvaging. Her reputation was in tatters, she had no finances and even more debts. If her smuggling past came to light, her liberty would be under threat. Nikolas was angry enough with her to investigate her farm finances and what would happen then?

It was all such a mess but if she had Sam, she could deal with anything. Without him…Esta didn't even wish to contemplate that. Her mind went blank every time she imagined her life without him in it. Perhaps a move to another city would make it easier to bear the grief. Even as she had the thought, she knew she could never leave her mother or her employees.

There was a knock at the door and, stupidly, her heart started to pound. She took a deep breath, put down her embroidery and went to answer it.

Sam stood without, freshly shaven, his hair cut and combed, wearing soft grey breeches and a white shirt. Her heart doubled its pace.

"May I come in?"

"Of course." She stood aside for him to enter. Her stomach flipped as he brushed past her, but he continued to the fire. She closed the door, resting her forehead against the cool wood. Was this the moment when he would reject her once and for all? She drew in a long breath and turned to find him studying her, the green of his eyes brilliant and compelling. Had there ever been a man so splendid? She couldn't remember meeting anyone who could rival him in looks, physique or sheer magnetism.

She took herself in hand. There was absolutely no point worshipping Sam if he was preparing to set her free. She drew herself up and looked him in the eye. "You've been busy since we arrived yesterday." She couldn't help the accusing tone.

He shook his head. "I thought it best to stay away. Away from temptation, you know. But I couldn't do it. I had to see you. See if what we have is what I think it is."

His words were frank and exposed so much of his insecurity she was astounded. "I doubted you. I've longed to speak with you, to hold you, but you've been so aloof. I was so desperately afraid…"

He crossed the room, wrapped her in his arms and pulled her so tight to him she could hardly breathe.

"My darling Esta," he said, "I'm sorry I gave you cause to doubt. It's a weakness I have… I believe no one will truly love me. I had no intention to hurt you."

He held her face between his hands, his gaze feasting on her eyes and then her mouth. She watched mesmerized as his lips lowered to hers; there was no more thought as he swept her away on a wave of pure pleasure.

She gave herself up to him as she had wanted to do on the ship. He was the master and she, his willing servant. The thought didn't sour her as once it might. He was all hands: in her hair, over her breasts, brushing her nipples and ensnaring her waist to pull her against him. He was hard for her and Esta could wait no more. She needed him inside her and there was no time to lose.

"*Now*, Sam, I've waited for you. It's been so long."

He caught her up and carried her through to the bedroom and the big bed where she had been so alone. He laid her down and lit a candle on each side of the bed. The warm glow burnished his skin to gold, and she licked her lips. His eyes followed the movement of her tongue, but he seemed in no hurry ...

"Sam!"

He grinned and unbuttoned his shirt as he stalked her, his eyes never leaving hers. By the time he knelt over her, her breath came in quick gasps. His gaze took in her state, her heaving breasts, nipples so tight it was almost painful.

Esta imagined he could smell her arousal. Perhaps he could, the way his nostrils flared. He was wild, untamed and she the prey, so different to the way she normally viewed herself - a capable, feisty woman who could order her own life.

She sat up and reached behind her to undo the many buttons down her back, but only had three undone before he grasped the collar of her gown and ripped it all the way down the back. Covered buttons flew everywhere, and she gasped, her feminine parts saturated with desire. She was naked beneath the gown. It was so thick and tight that no undergarment was necessary. He took full advantage, his large hands cupping her breasts, the weight of his body easing her back on the pillows.

His mouth found her nipples, first one then the other, and she almost leapt off the bed, her body arching into his. He did splendid things with his tongue, licking and flicking her aroused peaks. A pressure mounted, low down in her stomach, and tingling began in her mound. It was marvelous and exciting and oh!

She had to have him before it was all over and he refused her again. She had to find a way to push him over the edge, send him mad with desire.

His breathing was fast and hard, his pupils huge with only a thin rim of brilliant green framing them. "You drive me wild, Esta. When I'm with you I lose myself. Nothing else seems to matter."

That was good, very good, she thought, as she reached for his breeches and undid them. When she pushed them down, he sprang free and she gasped. *Can I take all of him inside me?* He raised her chin so he could look into her eyes.

"Don't be afraid, my love. We'll go slowly. This is the most natural act in the world. Relax and feel!"

He stripped off the rest of her gown until she lay naked. His eyes took her in, including the thatch of chestnut hair between her legs - the place that ached for him. He took his breeches off then spread her legs. She moaned as he ran his fingers lightly across her throbbing flesh.

Sam gasped as his fingers brushed the hard nub that pulsed at his touch. She threw her head back and moaned as the pressure mounted - sweet, sweet torture. It pushed at her, harder and harder and when his fingers dove inside her, she was lost into a maelstrom of sensation.

She knew nothing else until he nibbled his way from her navel all the way to each nipple. Everything inside her awoke. This time when he pushed her legs aside it wasn't his fingers that entered her. She gasped as his manhood nudged at her entrance, questing, exploring the hot slick depths hidden within her folds. She held her breath, not sure what to expect.

He was gentle, entering her by small pushes, waiting for her to stretch then thrusting again. At every push he moaned, until she couldn't hold her eagerness inside any longer. She thrust and he slid further in, stretching her almost to the point of pain.

"You're so tight," he said, "and this is so good."

Esta thought he had fully inserted himself, but he pushed once more and there was a sweet pain. She cried out but, when he would have stopped, she urged him on, gripping his backside so he couldn't pull away. His response was strong thrusts that took her higher, back to that glorious place where the world ceased to exist and only tumbling, swirling sensations were reality. She was vaguely aware of him stiffening on top of her and his seed pumping within. Again, he brought her back with his mouth on her breasts.

"You're so beautiful and sensual," he said. "You came apart under me. You can't imagine what that does to a man. To know I can do that to you. I'll never get sick of it."

She didn't wish to return to reality, just wanted to float on this raft of desire and sensation forever. "Do we have to talk? Can't we do that again?"

He laughed. "If you insist, my love."

The glorious rays of the sun woke Esta the following day. By their intensity, it was midmorning. She sat up and the blankets fell away. She glanced down at her bare breasts and encountered Sam's tanned back.

"Oh!" The night flooded back to her and her body heated. She was sore down below but not too sore for a repeat performance. The experience had been nothing like her mother described. There was so much pleasure involved, she worried at one point that she might die of it. Perhaps she was one of the lucky ones. She walked her fingers up his back, trying to wake him.

"Good morning, love," he said.

She so liked the sound of his voice, especially when he called her love. She could get used to that. For once in her life, someone was looking after *her*.

"Good morning," she said, snuggling down beside him. "Are you too tired for a repeat performance?"

He rolled onto his back and groaned. "Woman your stamina amazes me. Aren't you sore?"

"A little," she said, "but it was so nice."

"Nice! I hope it was better than that!"

"You know it was." She kissed him on a nipple and it instantly pebbled. His rod bounced under the blanket. "I see someone else wants more too."

He hauled her onto his chest and gazed up into her eyes. Her chestnut hair cascaded over his chest and neck. "I love your hair," he said, running his fingers through it. "You should wear it down so I can fondle it whenever I like."

"There's so much more of me you can fondle, pirate," she said.

He frowned.

"What's wrong?"

"I don't like you calling me that. It reminds me of a past I want to escape."

"Then I won't use it unless I'm angry with you," she said, smiling.

That didn't cheer him up as she had hoped. "Talk to me."

"I want this to be over," he said, serious green eyes, trapping hers. "I want us to start a new life together and put all that sordid mess behind us."

Esta shrugged. "I wish for that too and I've done all I can to make that happen."

"I know you have, I just …I'm afraid."

She drew him close. "There's no need. We can conquer anything."

"Easy words to say," he said. "I have so much more to lose now than I ever did. I find I'm not prepared to give any of it up." He swallowed hard and she wanted to protect him so nothing could ever hurt him again.

There was a knock on the outer door. Esta pulled on a robe and went to answer it. Merielle was without.

"The rider has come with word from the king," she said. "Nikolas has asked that you present yourself in the dining room in an hour. I have tried to find Samael but with no luck. Would you be able to tell him the news?"

She nodded. "I'll tell him if I see him. Thank you, Merielle."

The woman hesitated then turned and left. She wondered what else her beautiful friend had wished to say. Things between them hadn't been the same since Esta raced off, leaving Reid at the altar. It saddened her to lose that closeness but what choice had she had? To stay and commit to a life with Reid when she had deep feelings for another man? It wouldn't have been fair to Reid and in time he and Merielle would see that - she hoped.

She went back to the bedroom but when Sam held out his arms, she shook her head. "We must rise. The rider has come from the king and Nikolas wishes to see us within the hour." Her heart ached at the mixture of fear and hope in his eyes, but she squared her shoulders and lifted her head high. "We shall meet the news with courage and deal with whatever comes. It's all we can do."

* * *

Sam fastened the black ribbon at his throat and stood back to examine the black breeches and dark grey tunic Nikolas had loaned him. The Goddess only knew where his own clothes were. It had seemed an unimportant matter when in prison. He nodded at his reflection. The tunic was a little too broad across the shoulders but otherwise he could pass for a gentleman. There were still shadows beneath his eyes from the sleepless days in prison. He had lost weight and strength, but he liked to think his spirit was still strong.

All he was doing was putting off the inevitable. Nikolas had news from the king, and it was time to find out the verdict. He said a quick prayer to the Goddess and left the room.

He met Esta in the hallway. She wore the emerald dress she had worn to the ball and looked breathtaking. It said a lot about her nerves that she wore the gown. He suspected she used the dress as a kind of armor. Or perhaps it was to remind Nikolas that she was a member of the court, albeit a lesser member.

He smiled and took her hand which trembled. "You said all would be well, remember? Take your own advice." He placed her hand on his arm and turned to continue down the hall.

"Sam, wait."

When he glanced at her there were tears in her eyes. "What is it?"

"Last night was the most marvelous night of my life," she said. "I wanted you to know that. I love you, no matter what happens."

What had he done to deserve this amazing woman? "I love you too, Esta. What a wonderful team we'll make." Her smile lit up her face and it was one of the most joyful sights he had ever witnessed. He leant toward her and kissed each cheek. "Keep the faith," he whispered.

She nodded and they walked with quiet dignity, each caught up in their own thoughts, until they reached the dining room. Nikolas stood by the fire reading a sheet of parchment. Sam cleared his throat as they entered the room.

Nikolas turned. "Good day to you both. Won't you please take a seat?"

He looked down his nose. "I prefer to stand."

Esta squeezed his hand and he glanced down at her to see tears. She chewed her bottom lip.

"Get this over with, Cosara," he said.

"Very well." Nikolas looked down at the missive in his hands, took a deep breath and began to read.

"*His Majesty Benial Jazara, King of Thorius, makes this declaration regarding the sentence of Samael Delacost who has been convicted of piracy and treason. It will be stated that the death sentence is not appropriate in this case as the man has familial connections to the nobility. Therefore, in Delacost's case, I must order a different punishment.*"

Nikolas paused, his free hand tapping out a rhythm on his thigh.

"*I sentence Samael Delacost to hard labor for ten years. It is to be under the supervision of Nikolas Cosara, for the admiral to decide what tasks are suitable. Delacost is not to leave the admiral's side and must complete any chore asked of him. There will be no reduction in sentence but if Delacost should abuse the kindness of the Crown, his sentence may be doubled, and prison would be considered.*"

"I'll be a virtual slave!" Sam said, glaring at his brother.

"You think I want this?"

"Yes, I believe you do," Sam said.

"You think I want you under my nose night and day, constantly worried about what you might do next to bring me down?"

"I think you're very capable of making your own life a misery, Cosara," Sam said. "I hear you've been good at it in the past."

"You leave the past out of this," Nikolas snapped, gesturing with the king's letter.

"Why?" Sam stalked closer to his brother. "You have scandal in your past and want everyone to forget. How can they when your black sheep brother has turned up?" As he churned through the thoughts in his head, he realized it would suit Nikolas's career much better to be rid of him altogether. "Perhaps you don't want this after all. Perhaps you want me to go away and to never have to think of me again."

Nikolas nodded. "Perhaps I do."

"Lord Cosara, you can't mean that," Esta said, stepping forward.

The look Nikolas turned on Esta almost earned him a fist in the face from Sam. "I won't deny Delacost has been an irritation and you, Lady, are just as bad. My life was challenging before you both walked into it. Lately, it's been damned nigh impossible."

"Then we have a problem, Admiral." Esta folded her arms across her chest.

"Stay out of this, Esta," Sam said, and turned to Nikolas. "Your suggestions?"

"I've had an hour to think about how I'll deal with this and I've come up with nothing. There isn't any room to misunderstand this order. You'll stay with me wherever I go. The king has given both of us a ten-year sentence. Now get out of my sight, I need to think."

"Keep a civil tongue in your head!" Sam couldn't let this opportunity pass. He had to build bridges. Trouble was, Nikolas appeared to have dug his heels in. "I could agree to stay out of your way as much as possible. I give you my word I'll serve every day of that sentence."

Nikolas's eyes were wide, his mouth hung open. "You're considering this farce?"

"I don't have any choice. It's that or prison."

"Well, I do have a choice. I don't have to endure you under my nose every waking moment!"

"I can hear you both from the other side of the house." Merielle entered and closed the door behind her. "What will the servants say?"

"You've come a long way, my dear, if you're now worrying about our help!" Nikolas said, earning a gasp from Esta.

Merielle's eyes turned as hard as green flint. "That remark is beneath you, Nikolas, and I don't deserve it."

Nikolas sighed and walked over to her, catching her hand and kissing it.

"You're right and I'm sorry. I'm just so frustrated."

"Can you not accept Samael into our family and make the best of this? You lost a brother. Perhaps this is your Goddess restoring Jon to you."

"We both know Delacost is not Jon and I'd thank you not to mention them in the same breath." Without a backward look, Nikolas stalked from the room

Merielle stared at her hands for a long moment and when she looked up, there were tears in her eyes. "I should have known that would upset him. Why am I so stupid?"

Esta approached, tentatively laying a hand on Merielle's arm. "He misses his brother very much. Jon was lost at sea. Is that why he has such a violent reaction to Sam? Because Sam is from the ocean, too?"

Merielle shook her head. "That is only a small part of it."

"He doesn't think I'm good enough to be his brother." In his gut, Sam knew that was true, but it hurt to admit it.

Merielle looked upon him with sad eyes. "I can't deny that may be true, Samael, but mostly Nikolas is upset because he misses Jon. He is not ready for anyone to replace him. He may never be."

"Well, I won't spend the rest of my life trying to live up to Niko's idea of the perfect brother."

"You will not have to," Merielle said. "I believe he will soften in time. You must try hard to crack that shell he has built around his heart. Once you break through, he is a wonderful man."

"You speak from your experience," Esta said. "But I have my own concerns. Your husband blames me for being in this predicament."

"Not without reason," Merielle looked her in the eye every pore oozing disapproval.

"What would you have done?" she asked. "If Nikolas was in trouble, wouldn't you do anything to help him?"

Merielle frowned. "You could say I have already been in that position and yes, I did all I could."

Esta seized Merielle's forearms. "I love Samael. He was in danger and I did the only thing I could to save him. Don't condemn me for an action you would likely have taken yourself!"

He held his breath. This woman was critical to his future with Nikolas. If they could win her over, it would be easier for everyone. Merielle pulled her arms from Esta's grasp and walked over to look at the sketches on her side table. She picked up one of a man and woman and ran her finger down the woman's face.

"Family is important to Nikolas, but he needs time to form a relationship with you. Now he will have that time. It just remains to be seen how this can work." She turned to Esta. "As for you, Esta, you have an estate to run. I don't see where you fit into Samael's life of servitude to Nikolas."

Esta looked at him and they shared a smile. "I don't care how I'll fit. I only care that Sam is safe, with a chance for a new life. For he has given me a new life and it's the one I always craved but never believed existed. He is everything to me and nothing will be too difficult to bear with him by my side."

Sam joined her and enfolded her in his arms. "I can't fathom how I was lucky enough to find you after all these years," he said, for her ears only. "Please say you'll marry me. The rest we'll work out as we go."

She leaned back, tears in her rich brown eyes. "I'll marry you Samael Delacost and I'll love you until death and beyond."

He pulled her close and kissed the lips that had drawn him from the start. When he raised his head, they were alone. "Let's take this somewhere else," he said, and she laughed.

The sound was joy to his heart and he knew that, with Esta, there would be no more dark days.

EPILOGUE

ESTA sat by the fire in her chamber on the Cosara estate, full of dreamy contentment and not a small amount of excitement. She awaited the return of Sam from his voyage with Nikolas. That wasn't to say the last three months had been perfect. Far from it. Soon after the king's declaration, Nikolas had taken Sam to sea on a secret mission. Esta suspected it might involve the Sis Lenweri. She'd been anxious; worried as to how Sam fared with Nikolas and about the dangers of the voyage.

She knew too well how the sea could take a life. How it could rise from a mill pond to a raging beast and capsize a ship in a matter of hours. That aboard that ship were two very experienced sailors calmed her only a little.

But she had stayed busy. As soon as the brothers cast off, Esta returned to her estate. She and Katrine had ridden for Shawmere with a small crew of sailors as escort. On the way, she stopped in Costa and introduced herself to Sam's parents. To say they'd been surprised to hear her news was an understatement. Esta hoped that one day soon, she could move them to her estate where they'd live a better life and see their son more often.

She retrieved a portion of Sam's loot in Costa and made for Shawmere where she took ownership of the beautiful *Dawn Lady*. Esta privately hoped Sam would be pardoned early and he could use the refurbished ship to run a legitimate trade up and down the coast. Being back on-board ship as they sailed home had blown away the last of her fear for the future. It had been a joyful trip, made more wonderful as she bonded with her sister. If not for the sea sickness that plagued her, the voyage would have been idyllic.

Dawn Lady now rested in Esta's secret harbor, awaiting her next voyage, and she couldn't wait to share her plans with Sam. With the booty, she had paid her staff what she owed them plus another month ahead and invested a goodly chunk in the gold market with Reid's assistance.

Yes, her life was full of promise when a mere three months ago it seemed nothing could go right. She smiled thinking of all she had to look forward to.

A knock on the chamber door startled her out of her musing. She flew to her feet and flung open the door. Sam waited in the hall, his hair longer and wind-tossed, a huge bouquet of roses in his arms.

She threw herself at him and he lifted her in one arm as he stepped through the door, nudging it shut with his foot. The flowers were discarded as he kissed her senseless. She forgot all that she wished to tell him in the delight of having him back in her arms. They hadn't even said a word to each other, just allowed their bodies to make up for the time spent apart.

When she came up for air, her head spun but he allowed her no respite. He backed her toward the bedroom, his hands all over her, making her needy and breathless.

"I have news, beloved," she said, finally coming to her senses enough to speak.

"We have two weeks to catch up on the news," he growled, kissing her again.

He picked her up without losing contact with her lips and deposited her on the bed. His eyes devoured her as he stripped from his naval uniform and kneeled over her. "I've missed you every day, so much I never thought I'd survive." He placed kisses over her neck and the slopes of her breasts. "You're so delicious. I forgot how beautiful you are." He captured her mouth and she arched against him, begging for the release she could only know in his arms.

His body shone with sweat in the candlelight and she thrilled to know she had him so off balance. Her hips bucked as his hand slid under her skirt and up the outside of her thigh. Before she could do more than moan, he had raised her skirts, parted her legs and surged into her, his rod immediately triggering her climax. He must have felt her clench around him for he pounded into her, reaching his completion only moments later.

Esta became aware of his lips on her neck as she returned from the stars. "I missed that, my love," she said. "To be one with you is a joy I could never have imagined before."

"The next will be slower," he said, his breathing ragged. "I just had to have you, had to reassure myself that I hadn't imagined it."

"I know exactly how you feel," she said, running her fingers across his chest.

His eyes were hot as they slid over her, taking inventory. His hands completed their own exploration, and her breathing hitched as his palm stopped over her belly. "Am I imagining it, or have you filled out a little just here?" He ran his hand in soft circles over her abdomen.

"You're not imagining it." She placed her hand over his.

His eyes met hers. "You're with child?"

She nodded, marveling he knew her body so well he could tell a child grew within. Her heart beat so fast she could barely catch her breath. "Are you happy?"

"Oh, Esta, you'll never understand how happy you've made me. I know things aren't perfect but to come home from three months at sea, desperate to spend time with you, and then to be told I'm to be a father…" There were tears in his emerald eyes. "I won't let you down and I'll try to be a good father to all of our children."

She ran her fingers through his hair. "I know you will. I can't wait to show you our son or daughter."

"Does Merielle know?"

"I wanted you to be the first, beloved."

He smiled. "Uncle Niko will be excited."

Her stomach churned. The one thing she had been dreading about Sam's return was the advent of Nikolas. "I hardly think my pregnancy will be a cause of celebration for the admiral."

He kissed her fingers and smiled. "Months at sea have forged a bond between us, love. He has come to see me as a friend, even confide in me at times. We've a long way to go but it's no chore being his lackey. He has relaxed a lot and I wouldn't be surprised to see his anger toward you diminished."

"We shall see."

It would be a long time before she could relax in Nik's presence. He'd made no secret of resenting her interference when she forced him to acknowledge Sam.

"Yes, we shall." He kissed her again, his hand over her stomach. She gasped at a stirring, a fluttering, in her lower abdomen.

"What is it?"

"Movement," she said, "in my belly."

"The babe?"

"I think he knows his papa is here." She threaded her fingers through his and brought his hand to her lips.

A smile lit up his face. "I like the sound of that…papa."

She pulled his face down and kissed him with all the love and devotion she felt. He was in the process of remaking himself for her and he'd be a marvelous partner.

"Stop daydreaming about your child," she whispered, "and make love to me."

Samael Delacost, once the most feared pirate on the ocean, did just that.

THE END

GLOSSARY

Places

Kingdom of Thorius (Thor- ee- us) -the kingdom of men which encompasses the king's seat of Wildecoast and the prince's seat of Brightcastle, along with other smaller towns

Wildecoast (Will – dee – coast) -the capital city perched on the top of a cliff overlooking the sea on the east coast of Thorius; climate is mild but windy

Brightcastle - large inland town surrounded by forests and farms, three to four days ride west of Wildecoast

Costa - a small coastal fishing village south of Wildecoast; Sam's base

Amitania (Am – it – ay – nia) or *Elvandang* (Elle – van – dang) in elvish - the deserted city north of the Usetar Mountain Range in northern Thorius; once a thriving city; disputed ownership between elves and man

Usetar Range (You – set – ar) -the mountain range running across the northern parts of Thorius

People

Lenweri (Len – weir – ee) -the elven people who are tall and elegant with black skin and pointed ears and mainly dark hair; live in mountainous forests north and west of Thorius, in places encroaching onto Kingdom lands; also known as dark elves

Sis Lenweri - the faction of dark elves that wishes to take the kingdom of Thorius back from men

Defender - a race of shapeshifters who are created to defend those in danger; they sense those in need of their help; a Defender can shift into animal form and the ability is inherited through family lines

Mer – the race of people who live in the sea; consisting of mermaids and mermen; mermen are created from the souls of sailors who are killed by mermaids

Characters

Esta Aranati (Esta Ar-An-art-ti) – noblewoman, head of her family and estate, which lies to the south of Wildecoast; heroine of **The Lady and the Pirate** and part time smuggler; alias Lady Moonlight

Samael Delacost (Sam-ale Del-a-cost) – pirate who plies his trade up and down the eastern coast of Thorius, also know as The Singing Pirate; he has a *Lenweri* crew and is hero of **The Lady and the Pirate**

Katrine Aranati (Kat-treen) – noble woman and younger sister of Esta Aranati; she is a witch and her alias is Lady Star; heroine of **The Master and the Sorceress**.

Merielle – mermaid who desires to be human; she has vibrant red hair and is not familiar with the ways of Thorian people; heroine of **The Lord and the Mermaid** and married to Nikolas Cosara

Lord Nikolas Cosara (Nikolas Cos-arra) – once captain in the King's Navy, now a recluse; he is cousin to Queen Adriana and the hero of **The Lord and the Mermaid**

Claus and Harah Delacost – Sam's parents; live in Costa

Stino, Lonso and Ice – Esta's crewmen

Nande (Nan-dee) – Sam's first mate; *Lenweri*

Reid Vetta (Reed Vet-tah) – Master goldsmith in Wildecoast and Esta's betrothed for a short time

Aunt Paurella (Poor-ella) – Esta's aunt, younger sister to Esta's mother and the Queen's Seamstress; lives in Wildecoast in the keep.

Tomas Henn - local nobility in Wildecoast and one of Esta's suitors

Piotr Zialni (Peter) – prince of the realm, the king's nephew and Esta's suitor

General Kain Jazara (Cane Jazz-arra) – once general of the King's Army and Nik's best friend

Lady Alique Zorba (Al-eek Zor-bah) – Ramón Zorba's younger sister and one of the queen's ladies-in-waiting

Princess Alecia Zialni (Al – ee – sha Zee – al – nee)) - the King's niece and daughter of Prince Jiseve Zialni who rules the principality of Brightcastle and is next in line to the throne. Alecia's story begins in **Princess Avenger** and continues in **Princess in Exile**.

Vard Anton - a shapeshifting Defender; army captain of Brightcastle in **Princess Avenger;** holder of many secrets; his story continues in **Princess in Exile**

Prince Jiseve Zialni (Jiss – eve Zee – al – nee) - next in line to the throne of Thorius, younger brother of the King, a widower; father of Alecia Zialni

Lady Benae Branasar (Ben-ay Bran-a-sar) – noble lady with an estate in Tylevia; heroine of **The Lady's Choice**; healer; now married to Ramón Zorba

*Ramón Zorba (*Rah – mon Zor – bah) - Lord of Wildecoast and squire to Prince Jiseve Zialni; his family have an estate south of Wildecoast; hero of **The Lady's Choice;** now joint Guardian of Brightcastle with Benae

King Beniel Zialni (Ben – ee – elle Zee – al – nee) - King of Thorius; lives in Wildecoast; older brother of Jiseve Zialni and uncle of Alecia Zialni; married to Adriana

Queen Adriana - wife of the King; lives in Wildecoast; Alecia's aunt; Nik's cousin

Doctor Achan Mosard (Uck - ahn Mow - sard) – court physician in Wildecoast

Jon Cosara – Nik's younger brother; disappeared at sea

Saniste and Vitavia Cosara – Nik's parents

About the Author

BERNADETTE Rowley is a lover of epic fantasy who is a veterinarian by day and an author by night. She is currently published in the genre of epic fantasy romance with eight books, all set in her fantasy world of Thorius.

When she was a young teenager, an aunt gave her a copy of The Sword of Shannara by Terry Brooks and Bernadette has lived in various fantasy worlds ever since. It's no surprise that her chosen genre when writing romance is fantasy.

"I can see these settings so vibrantly in my mind and hope my readers can too."

But Bernadette has no desire to spoon-feed her readers by laboriously describing her fantasy settings. She would rather the reader use their own imagination a little.

Along with sword and sorcery, dashing heroes and stunning heroines, this author includes strong healing themes in many of her books - an element which is central to her everyday job.

"When I started writing the Queenmakers Saga, I never imagined my day job would force its way into my stories as it has."

And of course, there are animals, especially Bernadette's beloved horses.

Bernadette lives in Brisbane, Australia, with the four heroes in her life - her husband Michael and three grown sons.

Connect with the Author

Website: www.bernadetterowley.com
Facebook: www.facebook.com/bernadetterowleyfantasy
Twitter: www.twitter.com/bt_rowley